FOUR LEAF FELONY

A HOLIDAY COZY MYSTERY

BOOK ONE

TONYA KAPPES

TONYA KAPPES
WEEKLY NEWSLETTER

Want a behind-the-scenes journey of me as a writer?
The ups and downs, new deals, book sales, giveaways and more? I share it all! Join the exclusive Southern Sleuths private group today! Go to www.patreon.com/Tonyakappesbooks

As a special thank you for joining, you'll get an exclusive copy of my cross-over short story, *A CHARMING BLEND*. Go to Tonyakappes.com and click on subscribe at the top of the home page.

"What's wrong?" the flight attendant asked me. She put one hand on me when she noticed my knees were giving out, and with her free hand, she pulled the flight attendant seat down, easing me into it.

"I…" I gasped for air. "I…"

"You're having a panic attack. It's okay," she assured me, reaching behind her to get one of those throw-up bags. She put it in my hands. "Just breathe slowly in and out into the bag."

"No." I shook my head, trying to get away from the bag she'd shoved into my face. "Body. Body," I gasped and pointed to the bathroom. "There's—" I rolled my eyes up and tried to take a deep breath. "There's a body."

I pointed and gave up, resting my head back against the airplane's wall.

"Someone was in there?" She made an *eeck* face and smiled. "They probably forgot to lock the door. It happens all the time."

I reached up, grabbed the front of her uniform jacket, and dragged her down face-to-face with me.

"Dead body. Blood." It was all I could get out.

CHAPTER ONE

"And my daughter." Pride spilled out of the woman. Her smile, her eyes, her entire face lit up as she showed me the photos on her phone. One after the other she scrolled.

"She has three little children. Let me tell you"—she put her hand on her chest—"I never thought the girl was going to give me any grandbabies." She tapped the phone with her finger.

I slowly sucked in a deep breath, reminding myself that this was just a temporary situation. After the airplane landed, I'd never have to see this woman again.

"Look here." She shoved the phone in my face. "This is Joey."

I could practically smell the cookie he was holding in his picture. It was so close.

"He's a handful. He loves his mom. This is little Chance. He's a handful, but he loves his mom too." She scrolled past a few more until she landed on little Chance.

She'd done this photo dump on strangers a time or two. She did it flawlessly.

"This is my little Lizzy." The woman giggled. "She's just a doll baby. She's the cutest. Just the cutest," she repeated as if I'd not heard her say it the first time. "She's the cutest."

She stared at me.

"Oh." I realized she wanted a response. "Yes. She is."

She bragged on her three grandchildren, which I was far removed from. I mean, honestly, I had no idea what I was going to do for the rest of this four-hour airplane ride.

I knew I shouldn't have made eye contact when I first got on the plane. It was the eye contact that opened the flood gates of chatty granny.

The only hope I had was the connecting flight. What were the chances she'd be on that one and be seated next to me?

"Excuse me for a second. I had a little too much Diet Coke," I told her and unbuckled the safety belt.

"Airplane bathroom are awful. If you were my daughter, I'd told you to go to the bathroom before we got on the airplane." She wagged a finger at me. "You hold on. It's no fun squatting on that little toilet when there's turbulence." Her eyes grew with fear as though she had first hand experience.

"Thanks." I stood up and took a big deep breath before I took my first steps of freedom away from my seatmate.

This entire plane ride was nothing like I had in my head when I woke up. Really was anything ever turn out the way we imagined them?

There were things I needed to do to prepare myself for the biggest interview of my life. I would've loved to hear about little Lizzy and her brothers on any given day, just not today.

Today was the day I'd been waiting on for—well, I couldn't even remember how long. That was long if I couldn't remember.

"Get yourself together, Violet," I told myself under the fake smile as I stepped over a child playing in the aisle when the child should've been in a family member's lap. I tossed my long blond hair, which was perfectly styled today, over my shoulder.

Carefully I stepped over her.

"I'm sorry," a woman mouthed. She must've been the little girl's mom, they had the same eyes.

"No problem." I waved it off and continued down the center of the airplane toward the bathroom.

All eyes were on me. I'd been a reporter in my hometown of Normal, Kentucky for Channel Two news, where I also had my own show called "Good Day in the Park." I wrote a monthly column for my hometown newspaper, so I was used to the perfect smile.

I'd spent my career giving up any social life so I could get my one big break. This was it. Nothing was going to ruin it.

Just a few short days, you're gonna see me on TV, being a big-time reporter, I thought to myself when I noticed people glancing up at me.

Like my Aunt Lucinda told me, *Violet, honey, you've got to fake it until you make it.* That was exactly what I had done in Normal, and here I was —on my way to making it big!

The flight attendant was busy getting the little food cart ready to push down the aisle and stepped out of the way of the bathroom door when she noticed me going for the handle.

"Are you having a good flight?" she cordially asked. Her brown hair was parted to the side, pulled back into a low ponytail. The maroon uniform showed off a very appealing figure that showed she took care of herself. Something I could definitely understand.

It was one of the many things I needed to do to stay camera-ready at any moment.

"Yes. I am." I curled my fingers into the small opening of the handle and pulled the accordion bathroom door open. "Oh my gawd!"

My body shook. My breath heaved in and out at a rapid pace.

I slammed the bathroom door shut.

"What's wrong?" the flight attendant asked me. She put one hand on me when she noticed my knees were giving out, and with her free hand, she pulled the flight attendant seat down, easing me into it.

"I…" I gasped for air. "I…"

"You're having a panic attack. It's okay," she assured me, reaching behind her to get one of those throw-up bags. She put it in my hands. "Just breathe slowly in and out into the bag."

"No." I shook my head, trying to get away from the bag she'd shoved into my face. "Body. Body," I gasped and pointed to the bathroom. "There's—" I rolled my eyes up and tried to take a deep breath. "There's a body."

I pointed and gave up, resting my head back against the airplane's wall.

"Someone was in there?" She made an *eeck* face and smiled. "They probably forgot to lock the door. It happens all the time."

I reached up, grabbed the front of her uniform jacket, and dragged her down face-to-face with me.

"Dead body. Blood." It was all I could get out.

CHAPTER TWO

One Week Earlier

"One more week in this cold town is going to kill me," I told Gert Hobson, the owner of the only coffee shop in my small hometown of Normal, Kentucky.

Really, there weren't many shops and zero big-box stores. Some would say it was what made my hometown a tourist destination: the small shops and the locals, not to mention the Daniel Boone National Forest that curled up around the town like a hug from Mother Nature.

"The weather getting to you?" Gert asked. She flipped the switch on the coffee machine she used to make my special espresso combined with cocoa and ground chocolate and topped with steamed milk that delivered the best sweetness to my palate.

"No, though it has been unseasonably cold this winter." I leaned on the coffee shop's counter and drew my shoulders up to my ears when I twisted around and looked behind me at the line of customers in the cute coffee shop. "But I'm so tired of reporting on things like new trails discovered, all the reenactments, or how to be safe during the upcoming hunting season. I want to report on real things."

"What about 'Good Day in the Park'? Everyone loves it." Gert was trying to be nice. She always had that personality.

"You and the three others who watch it." I never told anyone in Normal how it was my segment and the station manager of Channel Two didn't give me my own cameraman. He'd told me it was my show and they didn't budget for any extra staff.

So to make me look better in front of everyone around here and get my own show, I paid for the cameraman out of my own pocket, making it look as though he was from the news station. He wasn't. I found him in the Help Wanted section for a videographer in the *Normal Gazette*, another place I did reporting just to make ends meet.

"I think you're selling yourself short." Gert frowned and handed me the coffee over the top of the glass display counter, where she kept the most delicious desserts. Some she made, and some were from the Cookie Crumble, the local bakery. "What do you want to eat? On the house."

"Nothing." I patted my stomach. "I've got to watch the calories for when I make it big."

I didn't dare think about the calorie content in the fancy coffee.

"Then your coffee is on the house." She looked past me to help the next customer in line.

I whipped around and knocked smack-dab into someone, spilling the hot drink down the camel-colored trench coat.

"Oh my gosh, I'm so sorry. I'm so sorry," I pleaded with the man and reached back around to get the towel Gert had extended over the counter. "You know what," I rambled and wiped the front of his coat down, seeing the stains of all of the delish contents not coming off. "I have a friend who owns a laundromat across the street. I can take your coat to her, and she'll have it all cleaned up in no time."

"Don't worry about it. It's fine." He smiled, and the creases around his eyes deepened. His brown hair was cut and blended better than Helen Pyle could do down at the Cute-icles Salon, Normal's only option to get a haircut. "I have another coat."

"I insist." I started to tug at the collar. "I'm not taking no for an answer. My mama taught me good manners, and it's just good manners for me to get your coat cleaned. What do you like to do? Hike? Kayak? Camp? Rock climb?"

"No. No. No." He shrugged off his coat. He was a well-to-do man with a blue button-down and the shiniest cufflinks I'd ever seen. "I'm passing through on my way to Tennessee to catch a flight back west."

"Flight?" I wondered, the journalist side of me. I was pleased as a peach with his coat in my possession.

"Yep. I was in Lexington doing some business, and my flight back to California got cancelled. They don't have any idea when the plane will leave. It could be a day or next week." He smiled. This time I noticed his dimples. "I'm a doer, which means I made other arrangements for a flight out of an airport in Tennessee. I was driving through your town and decided to grab me a coffee."

"Not wear one?" I joked.

"I don't think it looks good on me. Apparently you don't either, since you're so insistent on getting my coat cleaned. Which isn't necessary, seeing I've got to get going. I don't want to miss that flight." He tried to take his coat, but I held on to it. "Really. You don't need to clean it."

"You might'swell let her do it. Once Violet gets something in that noggin' of hers, she doesn't let go." Just hearing the voice of Dottie Swaggert before I saw her face made my stomach curl. "After all, she's failed at the other idea of getting out of this town. Can't you throw the gal a bone?"

"Dottie, go smoke a cigarette." I swiveled around and shot her a look before I turned back to him. He had a look on his face that said he was very entertained.

"A feisty go-get-it kinda gal." His lips drew up in a grin, and his head tilted with one big nod. "I like that in a woman. In fact, I came to Lexington to interview a woman who I thought had your gumption but disappointed since I didn't see that side of her. On television she comes off confident. In person, not so much."

"Television? Did you say television?" No wonder he was so fancy. He had to be a movie star. There were no shortage of them that came to

Normal to get away. In fact, a lot of movie stars loved to escape to the mountains in Appalachia, where they tended to be left alone.

"I'm not big-time." He held his hands out.

"I'm a reporter, so it got my interest. In fact"—I reached around and brought Dottie back into the conversation—"Dottie can tell you how I'm a big reporter for Channel Two as well as host my own show here in Normal called 'Good Day in the Park.' Right, Dottie?" I nudged her maybe a little too hard in the ribs.

"Mmmhmmmm," she ho-hummed. I had to do a double take when I noticed she'd already slipped a cigarette in the corner of her lips. It bobbled up and down as she spoke. "Yep. She's been trying to make me watch all them health segments she likes to do, but I think I'm just fine."

The man's eyes shifted to me like he was waiting to see if I was going to banter with her.

"As you can see, we have colorful citizens here in Normal, but I'm not planning on being here too much longer. I've got so many interviews with bigger markets, so I'm sure my time in Normal is limited." I lied but hoped he'd see something in me. "I'm Violet Rhinehammer, by the way."

I stuck my hand out from underneath his coat, which was folded over my forearm.

"Richard Stone." He stuck out his hand. "Violet. I like that name. Rhinehammer might not be a good stage name, but if you're willing to give up the name, I'm willing to interview you on one condition."

"What's that?" I gulped, trying not to show too much excitement.

"You have to fly to California to interview in one week." He looked down at the coat. "You can bring the coat with you then."

"She'd love to." Dottie reached around me and grabbed the card he'd taken out of his pants pocket. "We've been trying to get rid of her for years."

CHAPTER THREE

The more I recalled the morning where I thought my life had changed, the excitement, the phone calls I made to everyone and their brother, letting them know I'd made it to the big time, all started to pound down on my head like a gong.

A big one.

Or maybe the sudden migraine had to do with the dead body sitting just about three feet from me behind the little airplane accordion door.

"How are you doing, darling?" the flight attendant asked me like we'd just gotten back from taking a walk in the park or something so casual.

"How do you think I'm doing?" The bag I had still pressed up to my mouth muted the sarcastic tone of my question back to her.

The phone on the wall beeped, and she picked it up and gave all sorts of *mmhhhms* and *yes, okay, fine* to whoever was on the other end of the line before she hung up.

I kept my eyes closed, head down, and slowly tried to breathe into the bag. The heavy footsteps coming toward the back of the airplane made me look up.

"Hi there." The man had bent down between my legs. He couldn't've been any older than me. "I'm Jim Dixon, the pilot, and I understand there's been an issue."

"An issue?" I looked up at the flight attendant. "A dead body is not an issue. It's a murder, and someone on this airplane did it."

"Violet, right?" He looked up at the flight attendant. She nodded to confirm. "I do understand we have a deceased passenger confirmed, but we have no way of knowing how our passenger died."

"Yes. Yes, we do. Stab to the neck." I hung my tongue out for good measure. "And there's a killer on this airplane. Oh gawd. What if I'm next?"

The sudden realization of mortality started to set in.

"Where's my phone? I have to call my mom. I have to tell her I'm okay." I started to get up, but the heavy hand of Jim Dixon on my shoulder pushed me back down.

"This is what we cannot have on here right now. We are thousands and thousands of feet up in the air." He talked to me like I was a kindergartener. "And if you or anyone else goes around yelling about what you had seen behind the door, then we will have an airplane full of panicking people. And we don't want that, do we?"

Slowly he shook his head, and I mimicked him.

"Can I ask you to sit here while I take a look for myself? Not that I don't believe you, but I've got to make the decision on whether or not we make an emergency landing. Do you think you can stay calm?" Jim's tone was somewhat soothing and a bit comforting.

I nodded to confirm I could stay calm. Just to make sure, I put my head back between my legs and kept the paper bag over my mouth in case I started to hyperventilate again.

He patted my leg and stood up. Remember the sound of long fingernails running down a chalkboard and how the sound made goose bumps curl up your body? The sound of the folded slats of the accordion door sliding together when Jim pushed it open gave me the exact same feeling and chills.

There was a huge pause and silence that made me look up.

"Everything is fine, everything is fine," the flight attendant assured me, batting her long eyelashes. There wasn't a smile on her face to go with her words.

My gaze shifted from her to Jim.

"Cherise, there is a dead body in the bathroom." He said it like he wasn't expecting it. "We are going to need to land the plane."

"I told you." I couldn't help but confirm to him that I was right. "There's a killer here," I said with a hushed whisper out of the side of my mouth.

"And that is why we don't need to alarm anyone. You leave this up to me. Understood, Violet?" His face was so stern, as if something bad was going to happen if I didn't listen to him.

"Yes. Fine." I went back to the bag and couldn't help but hear that door unfold back to close.

There were some murmured words between Cherise and Jim, but I didn't bother trying to listen to them. My mind was preoccupied with telling my stomach not to throw up since my heart had pumped all the blood to it because of the panic attack I was having. I knew if I stood up, my brain would be lacking oxygen because the heart was so selfish it took all the oxygen too.

Before too long, my organs and I were left in the back of the airplane with Cherise and the dead guy in the toilet.

Ding, ding. The chimes for the airplane's announcements were piped through the intercom system, followed up by the static noise of the cockpit before Jim's familiar voice came across.

"Ladies and gentlemen, this is Pilot Jim Dixon. I'm sorry to interrupt our flight. Unfortunately, we need to make a quick landing into the closest airfield in Holiday Junction." The rattle of chatter began to fill the inside of the airplane. "Cherise will be coming down the aisle to collect any garbage you may have. Please put up your tray tables and bring your chairs to an upright position. We will be landing shortly and be there for a small amount of time before we take off to our destination of sunny California."

"Trash? Trash? Trash?" Cherise's happy tone had a nervous click to it as she asked each passenger row by row. "I'm sorry. Do you think you can turn around and buckle up? We are descending." Her voice was becoming much harder with each passenger she had to tell to turn around.

People started twisting around, and chatter continued to fill the cabin of the airplane. All of a sudden, when I looked up, eyes were all on me.

"I think she's sick. That's why we are landing," I overheard someone say.

Cherise gave up and came back with an empty garbage sack.

"What about the family? What about his family? Somebody has to be on board." My mind was racing.

The phone buzzed again.

"Mmhmmm. Hold on." Cherise put the phone to her chest. "Do you think you could peek in there and see if you can find some sort of identification on him?"

"You want me"—I pointed to myself—"to go in there"—I moved my finger to point to the accordion door—"and rummage through his pockets to see if I can find any ID on the dead man?"

"Dead man?" I heard someone ask. "Did she say dead man?" The person in the row just in front of the bathroom turned just enough around the corner to look at me. "Did you say 'dead man'? Is there a dead man in there?"

"Everything is fine. Just fine." Cherise didn't sound so convincing. She used her finger to gesture for the passenger to turn around. "We will be landing soon. Please turn around."

"I overheard you telling the woman you were sitting with that you were some fancy reporter." Cherise had bent down and was whispering into my ear. "What more of a story do you need than this? So get in there and find out the information. Just think about it. You get the big scoop before the police even get it."

Boy oh boy. Cherise sure did know how to dangle a carrot in front of my nose.

CHAPTER FOUR

I t was like a movie. The eerie music played in my head. Suddenly there was voiceover too.

Violet Rhinehammer hit the big time, and it was nothing like she expected. The small-town Kentucky girl had her hopes set on interviewing for a big television network. Little did she know, her quick-witted reporting while on an airplane when a passenger was murdered would not only show the world what a gift she was, but she'd get her own reporting talk show.

The idea of just how big this could be for my career washed over me as I gripped the handle of the accordion door to prepare myself to get in, get the wallet, and get out.

In one fluid motion, I ripped the door open. The man's eyes were open, staring at me, and the knife glistened.

"Nope. Can't do it." I shut the door and began to heave between words like a child with a bad case of the stomach flu. "No." My gag reflex had me sticking my tongue out. "Bag." I reached out for the paper sack. "Bag," I gagged out the word before I almost lost my cookies.

"Some reporter you are. What are you the reporter for, the first day of kindergarten?" Cherise tossed me the bag. "Girl. If you're going to make it big, you're going to have to get some tough skin. Those looks, fake lashes, and pearly-white smile aren't going to get you far."

"I'll show you," I muttered into the bag and kept my head down until the wheels of the airplane bounced on the pavement, signaling touchdown.

I kept my head forward when the overhead bells dinged to let us know the plane had come to a complete stop. The sound of people unclicking their seat belts echoed throughout the cabin, and people jumped up to get a good, long stretch. Little did they know why we were here. A few of them looked back at me as if it were my fault we landed in Holiday Junction.

I shoved my hair behind my head and straightened up my shoulders. *I am a reporter*, I reminded myself. *I am supposed to do hard things.* I continued to pump myself up. Besides, who was going to do it for me now that I was on my own adventure?

Granted, it was just an interview for the job, but I needed to start now even if no one was ever going to see my heroic act.

I collected myself, as my mama would tell me to, and stood back up, handing the bag to Cherise. Again, I reached out, gripped the handle, and ripped the door open. I kept my eyes on the man's pocket. There was a hint of a leather edge sticking out of it.

"Gloves. I need gloves." I put my hand out for Cherise. "Gloves, Cherise. We can't mess up any evidence."

A sly smile crossed her lips. Quickly, she turned on the plastic soles of her shoes, which I'd never be caught dead in, and whipped open a cabinet. She pulled a first aid kit out, opened it, and scoured through it until she found a pair of gloves.

There were some rumblings going on in the front of the airplane, and without paying any attention, I slipped my fingers through the holes of the gloves and sucked in a deep breath. With the vision of my gorgeous hometown with the backdrop of the Daniel Boone National Park in my mind to distract me from the actual scenery, I carefully reached between the man and the wall, where I grabbed the tip of the wallet.

"Got it!" I held it up like I'd won something where I got a trophy. "Got it."

"You did!" Cherise's excitement mirrored mine. Both of us squealed.

"Thank you, ladies." The larger-than-life deep voice came from behind us. "I'm
Chief Matthew Strickland with the Holiday Junction police department. You can join the other passengers in the airport while we assess the situation. We will be taking statements inside."

He stepped aside, planted himself next to the aisle, and gestured for us to leave the airplane.

I gulped and did what he'd told us to do. A few more men in uniform made their way to the back of the airplane, stepping aside for me and Cherise to continue down the aisle.

"Did you get the information I asked for?" Jim Dixon stood in the doorway of the cockpit just like he would do at the end of any flight.

"Oh, yeah." I looked down, remembering I had the wallet of the dead man. "I'll take it back to Chief Strickland."

I moved my way around Cherise and made my way to the back of the plane, but not without first opening the wallet.

Inside there was a driver's license behind the clear plastic film. It showed a man with a big smile and black hair that could've been brushed before the photo, but that didn't matter now.

Jay Mann.

I snapped the wallet shut and held it out.

"I took the wallet out of his pocket." I handed Chief Strickland the leather wallet, which just so happened to be very high quality.

"You disturbed the body?" he asked.

"No. No." I shook my head. "I was very careful. Even wore gloves. See?" I lifted my gloved hands in the air, wiggling my fingers.

"Interesting." His eyes lowered, as did his voice. "I think I want to talk to you first."

"Great. My name is Violet Rhinehammer. I'm a reporter." I proudly stated my job. "I'm on here going to a big interview out west. Which makes me wonder, how long do you think you'll take to get the"—I clicked my tongue and nodded my head sideways toward the bathroom —"body out so we can get on our way?"

I made a little whistle with my mouth and used my finger to mimic an airplane taking off.

"Seeing how this is a crime scene, it looks like you'll be grounded here for a few days. You might want to give your possible new employer a little phone call letting him know you're to be a few days late." It was as if he was mocking me and taking pleasure in telling me that my big break was on the brink.

"Days?" I questioned. "I don't have days."

"Ms. Rhinehammer, please exit the airplane. I'll be with you shortly." He turned his back to me, leaving me feeling infuriated and, well, just about beside myself.

I stalked down the aisle and found myself standing on a small metal platform with about ten steps that took me down to the runway.

"Great." I stood there and looked around, knowing this was not how I pictured the end of this flight. I pulled my phone out of my pocket and thumbed through the call log to find the number of Richard Stone.

"Have you landed already?" Richard asked.

"You're not going to believe this." I proceeded to tell him as I took the steps one by one, careful to not get my heels caught.

"Violet." He sounded very serious. "This is going to be your interview. I'm asking you to go live right now. We can dial you into the station, and you can bring us an update. We will get a leg up on all the national networks with this breaking story."

"Breaking story?" I asked.

"Yes. Murder in the sky." He said it like it was some big headline. "This is going to get you on the map, and if it's big enough, you're automatically hired. Starting salary is two hundred thousand dollars."

"How do I get dialed in?" There was no doubt this was my big break. For a second, I felt like I should thank Jay Mann, but I didn't. Instead I said a little prayer for him and his family, wherever he was from.

CHAPTER FIVE

"Violet, can you have someone hold the phone while you do the broadcast? Do you have some earbuds you can put in?" Richard Stone kept me on the phone. "It's important you get this story, and now. There's word on the line that there's been a murder on board a domestic flight. You're there. You were on it."

"Cherise." I grabbed her as soon as she walked through the terminal doors from the runway. "I need you to hold the phone for me."

"Are you joking? I'm not your assistant. I'm going to give the officer my statement then go to the hotel, where I'm going to knock back a few." She waved her finger at me. "You should too. From what I was just told, we are going to be here a few days."

"Few days?" I bit my lip. It was even more crucial than before that I get the shot and seal the deal before Richard heard I might be stuck in Holiday Junction. "You have to do this. You owe me. I went in and got the wallet. I'm doing a live shot for my job, and I am the only one here to do a live, which means my footage will spread all over the world as the reporter who broke the story. I will tell them how I did all the work to find out who this man was and let them know how you refused to go in there. How safe will that make this airline seem? A flight attendant refused to help during an emergency."

"You wouldn't." She gasped.

"Try me." I wiggled my freshly plucked brows.

"Fine." She huffed and grabbed the phone from me.

"Thank you." I looked around for the best possible place to shoot the live and noticed a wall filled with four-leaf-clover cutouts next to the huge window where you could see the entire airplane, from which they'd yet to take out the body. "That's cute."

I'd almost forgotten we were coming up on St. Patrick's Day, but this place looked like it was the St. Patrick's Day headquarters.

"Over here," I told Cherise and had her follow me to the wall. Out of habit, thank goodness, I was able to put my earbuds into my ears and talk to Richard. "Richard, I'm ready."

Richard gave me all sorts of instructions on how to tap into the studio's network, which magically let me stream straight into the newsroom.

"And this is going to secure my spot on the news team?" I wanted to make sure.

"This is one heck of an interview that would be hard to beat." He made me feel so much better about my decision to pack my bags and follow my dream. "We are going live in three, two."

Before he said one, I handed the phone to Cherise.

"This is Violet Rhinehammer. International Correspondent." I smiled into the phone and did my best not to sound like a hick. I had been able to use my on-air personality voice, but when I was all aflutter, that southern twang just came out of me, and nothing was going to reel it in. "I'm coming to you live from—" I stopped talking because I'd forgotten where we had made the emergency landing.

"Holiday Junction." Cherise peeked over top my phone.

"Holiday Junction, where there's been an emergency landing. The information I'm about to tell you is not for younger ears, so now is the time for them to leave the room. This information has not been confirmed by law enforcement, but I can confirm that I've seen it with my own eyes, as I was a passenger on the airplane." I felt like my explanation took enough time for anyone with children watching to get their children out of earshot. "There has been a murder on the airplane. I can confirm this because I bravely went into the bathroom to retrieve the man's information, which I will not disclose at this time, due to the fact I'm not sure if his family has been notified."

"Violet, send me the information, but for now, sign off and tell the world you'll be back. Good job." Richard was in my earbud.

"Again, there has been an emergency landing here in Holiday Junction because I discovered a murdered body. This is an unfolding situation. This is Violet Rhinehammer. I'm reporting to you live at the scene because no other news channels can get through security to get this up-and-personal broadcast to you." The confidence was bubbling up in me as I found my footing with talking into my phone, and people started to gather around me.

They were watching me. They came one by one, standing in front of me as I found my strong voice.

"I will be broadcasting live footage and keeping you up to date." I reached out and grabbed the lady who had sat next to me on the airplane. "Can you tell me what you saw on the airplane?"

"What?" She looked at me. "Honey, I don't know if you are tick-tocking or whatever it is you young people do, but we are watching them bring out the body."

With big eyes, I looked back at Cherise. She was rolling her hand for me to keep talking after I'd realized the crowd wasn't watching me broadcast. They were watching out the window behind me.

Chief Strickland had one end of the black bag while another guy had the other end. They had to carry the body down the steel steps, and there was another person waiting for them at the bottom with a gurney.

"As you can see, they have now de-planed the body." I took the phone from Cherise and held it up to the window. I had pinched in a closer shot when I noticed Chief Strickland had taken a phone call, and for a few short seconds, he looked my way.

"Get off that phone!" he mouthed and pointed to me. "Hang up the phone!"

"You better do what he wants you to do, or he might take you to jail," the woman who sat next to me warned.

I turned the phone around to me and said, "This is Violet Rhinehammer. International reporter."

I clicked off just as several messages from friends back in my hometown of Normal, Kentucky came through by text.

"I see you're making quite a fuss." A man in a security uniform sidled up to me.

"Who wants to know?" I decided not to look at the texts from the people from home since they'd never really seemed to think I was going to make it big, and here I was on the national news.

"I'm Rhett Strickland, and I was told by that guy." He pointed past me out the window. I followed his finger and noticed Chief Strickland standing with his legs apart, his hands fisted on his hips, his eyes staring right at me.

"Chief what's-his-name?" I turned back around and rolled my eyes. "There was a murder, and there's a murderer in this room." I lifted my finger in the air. "I'm a big-time reporter, and it's my job to keep the public informed." I looked at his uniform a little more closely. "What are you, a mall cop?" I shook my phone to his badge. "And is your name really Rhett?"

"I loved that movie." His dimples deepened. At one time, those dimples would've made me wobbly in the knees.

Not today. Maybe just a little weak when I took in his dark hair, olive skin, a face that should be in a magazine, and a body to match. They sure didn't build them like that where I was from.

"And I am the airport security, but Chief 'what's-his-name' is my uncle, and you are right about a murderer being in this room." He snatched my phone out of my hand. "And if you keep broadcasting all sorts of things happening with your amazing reporter skills on this thing, you're giving them all the details so they aren't on their toes."

He slid my phone into his other hand when I lunged forward to get it back.

"You see, if the murderer doesn't know what's going on, they get a little fidgety and nervous. Kinda gives himself away." He made a good point.

"Himself? We think it's a man?" I picked on this one little detail.

"Just the semantics of the word. Himself or herself. Either way, it's not gender specific." He let out a long sigh. "Are you one of those reporters?"

"One of those?" I felt a smidgen offended. "I'm sorry if I've offended you"—I leaned in to look at his name again on the pin on his jacket— "Rhett Butler."

"Nope, not named after the movie character. It's a family name, and my last name is Strickland." The dimples faded. My phone beeped, and he looked at it. His dimples showed and deepened as he read my messages. "I'm guessing you don't look like this all the time?"

"Funny." I reached up and this time grabbed my phone.

"If we catch you doing another live broadcast or whatever it was you were doing to get on the national news, my uncle will lock you up for obstruction of justice." He gave me one last look before he snorted and walked away.

"At least I have my phone." I flipped a long strand of hair behind my shoulder. I decided to slide my phone open to read the texts.

"What is this?" I looked at the video text sent from Helen Pyle, my hairdresser from home.

Looks like you made it big-time, she texted along with a video.

I clicked the video. She'd sent me a link to my live broadcast.

Me.

The hair that I thought looked nice and neat, the makeup I'd carefully applied this morning before the flight, looked nothing like the image in my head of the person doing the reporting.

I gulped.

My hair was clumped in a few different places from my sweating, and my mascara had dripped down and dried on my face, making me look like an NFL football player. My fake lashes were half on.

"No," I gasped and frantically clicked over to social media.

Post after post was a photo of me standing in front of the four-leaf-clover wall and looking like the character the Joker.

Amateur reporter reports there's been a murder and looking for murderer. She looks like she killed someone. Honey, look in the mirror. You're giving yourself away.

I had become a meme.

CHAPTER SIX

"Oh, come on, don't be sore." Cherise had found it very amusing that I'd become a meme. "It's funny. Don't you have a sense of humor?"

"Not when it comes to my job. I am a professional and want to be taken very seriously." I was never so happy to give Rhett the Mall Cop my contact information so they would release us from the airport. "I just want to get to a hotel and get in bed. It's been a long day."

I gripped the hotel voucher they'd given the passengers.

We were standing outside the tiniest airport I'd ever seen. Literally you walked into the airport, and there was one person at a computer before Rhett let you through security into the one-room lounge before you exited the double slider doors to walk to the airplane.

I was guessing not too many people flew in or out of Holiday Junction.

We stepped outside, and there were mountains in the background on one side and flat land that led to the seaside area of Holiday Junction.

My phone vibrated, and I looked at it. My cheeks puffed up for a long exhausted sigh at seeing the battery level in the red.

"What now?" Cherise had stopped next to me, the pull-up handle on her luggage in her grip.

Somehow she'd been given access to take her things, but no one else was even allowed to think about asking for their belongings. Heck, she could've been the killer for all we knew. She was back there the entire time.

Hmmm, I thought to myself and wondered if my time here could be well spent doing my own investigation. Then I could do a huge segment on the national news where I'd be able to show those who mocked me on social media how I was a real investigative reporter.

"I should've put my phone charger in my purse, but I put it in my carry-on, which is on the airplane." I shoved my phone in her face. "I'm in the red. It won't make it until the morning."

"I don't have that type of phone, or I'd give you mine," she said with an empathetic smile on her face. "If it's any consolation, they are talking about leaving first thing in the morning."

"How am I going to know that if my phone is dead?" I asked and took a step back when a car came to an abrupt stop right in front of me, almost hitting me.

"I'm sure the hotel will have something for you."

The door of the car popped open. She hit the button on the handle of her luggage and pushed the handle down into the top before she picked it up and threw it in the back seat of the car.

"You got an Uber?" I asked and wondered how I was going to get to the hotel. "We can share. I can pay half."

"Uber?" She laughed. "You are so funny. I live here. Maybe you should be one of those comedic reporters on Saturday Night Live." She put her left foot in the car. "See you in the morning."

I leaned down to see who was in the car.

All I saw were big blue eyes staring at me and the back of Cherise's head because they were wrapped up in a big kiss.

"Ta-ta." Cherise's fingers drummed in the air before she tugged the door shut and the car zoomed off.

"Yeah. Ta-ta," I groaned, shaking my head as I watched the taillights fade off into the distance. "Now for a taxi."

"Taxi?" I looked up when I heard the voice next to me. I guessed I didn't realize how loudly I was talking to myself. "We don't have taxis in Holiday Junction. But we have scooters," Rhett continued.

He pointed to a row of battery-powered scooters.

"And you're lucky there's one over there, since I'm sure everyone is heading down to the Shamrock Parade." He seemed really happy about this parade. "It's the talk of the Village, and you certainly don't want to miss out while you're visiting."

"Is that right?" I asked, as thoughts of me on a scooter didn't seem so appealing. I almost corrected him to remind him I was not visiting, just passing through.

"I bet you can even get that fancy international news network to do a piece on Holiday Junction's St. Patrick's Day week of festivities while you're here." He shrugged. "Maybe you can even get a piece printed in the *Junction Journal*."

"The *Junction Journal*?" I snickered. "No thanks."

He didn't need to know how I'd just left a small town, and from what I could tell by how people were talking, Holiday Junction was much smaller than Normal.

"I don't plan on being here long enough to write any sort of piece for the paper." My tone softened. There was no need to be nasty to Rhett. He was trying to be helpful.

"It'll take a while for my uncle to sort through the mess. With limited officers due to the holiday, they are pretty short-staffed." He didn't bring me any sort of good news.

As hard as I tried not to show any emotions, since I was on the verge of crying, my brows bumped together in a scowl.

"Is there a lot of crime in Holiday Junction to warrant officers working a small-town parade?" I needed to know what I was dealing with here before I called Richard Stone to see exactly where he stood on my little unexpected trip to Holiday Junction.

"We are a village," he corrected me.

I rolled my eyes. "Village. Town. Potato. Potaaato." I gestured both hands in the air like a scale.

"Crime?" he asked, displaying a wide grin. "You don't get it. Today is a holiday, and most officers take the day off to be with their family and friends."

He unbuttoned his security guard shirt one button at a time. My eyes shifted away from him and back several times as I tried to figure out what he was doing.

"And if you'll excuse me, that's where I'm headed." He unbuttoned the final button and slipped out of the shirt, exposing the green T-shirt underneath with a huge white four-leaf clover on it. "You should come out of the hotel for some fun festivities. You have nothing else to do until Uncle Matthew takes your statement."

"There's been a murder." Did I have to remind him? "What kind of town am I stuck in?"

"Village," he corrected me. Again.

"I see you don't like what I just said." He grimaced in a "who cares" way, flipping the shirt over his right shoulder, where he was visibly flexing his muscles for me to see. "Either way, scooter or feet." His lips formed a thin line, and his head gave a quick tilt to the side before he waved goodbye.

My eyes burned watching him cross the street to the parking lot that serviced the small airport. He jumped in his car, slid back the convertible top, and headed the way he'd gestured for me to get to town as if he didn't have a care in the world.

My shoulders slumped, and my walk was slow on my way over to the scooter.

"My oh my, I'm being tested." I looked up to the sky and wondered if this was one of those times the interim preacher at the Normal Baptist Church, the church I had attended in my hometown, had talked about. The preacher would preach about being tested on our way to our purpose. "I'm up for a challenge to prove I do deserve to go to California and be on television."

Just as I made it to the last scooter, someone rushed around me and grabbed it right out from underneath me.

"Hey! I was going to use that!" I yelled after the boy, but he took off and didn't turn around. His hat was turned around backward, and it, too, had a shamrock on it. "I see that hat! These people are nuts."

I glared at the kid, who still didn't turn around, and noticed Rhett had stopped his car and put it in reverse. I looked down at my phone so he wouldn't see me looking at him.

"Great," I moaned after I noticed my phone had completely died. This day was turning out to be nothing like I had planned it to be.

I put my fists on my hips and let go of a deep breath in exchange for a cry.

He brought the car to a complete halt.

"I saw what happened. You snooze, you lose." Rhett patted the passenger seat. "What about a ride? I'm heading that way."

"No. I'm good. I can walk." I didn't know him from Adam. "Besides, I don't want to be the next murder victim your uncle has to investigate."

"Trust me, you aren't my type, and I'm only being friendly. Suit yourself." He shoved the gear shift back in drive.

The hearse rolled up, making me take a step back, and the sound of some squeaky wheels caused me to look back over my shoulder to the entrance of the airport.

They were bringing out Jay's body. I shuddered.

Everything happened so fast. They opened the back door of the hearse and pushed the gurney into the hearse before it zoomed off.

"Wait!" I called after the hearse when I noticed something had fallen from the gurney. It was a black silk pocket square with green four-leaf clovers imprinted on it, along with the stitching of the letters J and M. "His handkerchief fell out!" I waved it in the air.

Rhett was still parked as if he were waiting for me to jump in.

"Fine." I tucked the silk square into my purse and opened the car door. "You take me to the hotel, and that's it."

I knew if I could just get to the hotel, I'd be able to find the morgue, where I would give them the square.

Rhett gave me a cocky wink and confident smile that told me I was in trouble.

27

CHAPTER SEVEN

The wind whipped my long blond hair all around my face. Unsuccessfully, I tried to gather all of it up in my hand around my neck, but once I got a good handful started, the other side would fly up in the air.

Out of the corner of my eye I could see Rhett looking over every once in a while and smiling. I wasn't about to let him see how much his attitude infuriated me.

When I didn't see any sort of town, um, Village up ahead, my heart started to palpitate.

"Do you have a phone charger?" I asked Rhett.

"Help yourself." He lifted the console in between the seats with a free hand, and there was a cable hidden in there.

"I didn't think," I paused before I accidentally said town since he seemed very sensitive about it "Village was this far out. How much longer?" I asked, trying to keep a steady voice.

"It's been like three minutes." He said it just as we got to a sign that read "City Limits," right before a little bit bigger sign that read, "Holiday Junction: Celebrate Good Times."

"You like that." He'd noticed the grin on my face.

"It's cute. I guess it's interesting how you celebrate St. Patrick's Day.

I'm not Catholic, so I don't know a whole lot about St. Patrick." I shrugged and noticed the row of houses on each side of the street.

There were lights dotted along the sidewalk, with four-leaf-clover flags waving along with the slight breeze. There were large trees giving shade to the many people who were all walking toward what I'd guessed was the downtown area.

"Catholic? What does religion have to do with how we celebrate?" he asked.

"I'm just saying how you seem to go all out for St. Patrick's Day, but I guess Chicago turns their river green." My face reddened from embarrassment. "I was just saying..." I felt like I needed to clarify and not sound so, well, dumb.

"Do you celebrate Christmas where you're from?" he asked and beeped his horn after he stopped in front of one of the houses.

"Oh, where I come from, Normal, Kentucky, we love Christmas." My heart tugged at the thought of me not being there this Christmas since I was going to be living in California. I threw the emotion out of my head.

"Is it your birthday?" he asked.

"No. It's Christmas." I pulled my head back, and my eyes narrowed.

"If it's not your birthday, why celebrate?" he asked and this time gave the horn two quick beeps.

"You've gotten your point across. I'm sorry I offended you about St. Patrick's Day." I rolled my eyes and put my head in my hand as my elbow rested on the door of the car, my hair gathered in my grip.

"St. Patrick's Day?" His head laid back on the headrest of the car seat, he cocked his head to the side and gave a relenting stare. "Holiday Junction celebrates every holiday. It kinda sucked growing up because it's such a cliché, but as I got older, I watched tourists such as yourself come and their eyes light up. Gave them something inside."

"I am not a tourist. I am a victim that wouldn't even have known Holiday Junction existed unless there was a murder on the airplane." I heaved in a deep breath and kept my mouth shut.

What was this guy thinking?

"Why are we here?" I asked when he beeped again.

"For her." He sent a nod past me, and I turned to my right to see this woman coming out of the house we were parked in front of, wearing a lime-green scoop-neck three-quarter-length-sleeved tea-length lace dress. She had black hair pulled back into a neat bun on top of her head and large black sunglasses to hide her eyes.

She was tall—or at least the black high heels she wore made her appear taller than she probably was—but she was thin and very striking.

"Get out and let her in," he instructed me.

"Girlfriend?" I asked as she approached the car.

"Hardly," he muttered. "Hey, Fern. This is…" He appeared to have lost my name.

"Violet Rhinehammer. International news correspondent in town for the big murder." I thought it would grab her attention, but it didn't seem to faze her.

Out of the corner of my eye, I noticed Rhett had opened his mouth to correct me, but he snapped it shut.

"It looks like you could use these more than me." She tugged off her glasses and handed them to me. "Where'd you pick her up, Rhett?"

"Pick me up?" I darted the question to him and then looked at her as she got into the car and literally sat on top of the convertible top in the middle.

"Airport. Tourist who needed a ride." He shot me a look as if to tell me not to say a word about the murder.

That got my attention. There was something he did want me to keep to myself.

"We can talk later, Fern." He put the car in drive and started back down the road.

"What's the speed limit?" I asked when I noticed a couple of kids on the street had passed us on the bikes. "And isn't it dangerous for you to be sitting up there? Where I come from, it's illegal not to sit on a seat with a seat belt on."

I looked up when I heard a marching band playing just as we drove underneath the ladders of two firetrucks, one on each side, the Irish flag hanging from the extended ladder on one of the trucks and the American flag hanging down from the other fire truck.

"Elbow. Wrist. Wave." Fern had an exhausted tone in her voice as she waved to the crowd gathered along the road. "Where's the candy?" she asked Rhett.

"Violet, can you grab that bag of candy underneath your seat?" he asked.

"I'm in some sort of twilight zone." I blinked a few times when I realized we were part of a parade. "I thought you offered to take me to the hotel." I reached underneath my seat and pulled out a large bag of lollipops.

"I did. I just didn't tell you that I had to drive Miss Holiday Junction in the St. Patrick's Day parade on our way. The hotel is on the route." Without him even looking my way, I could tell he was enjoying every single bit of discomfort he was putting me through, and he was doing it on purpose.

"Elbow, wrist, wave," Fern kept repeating behind her fake smile as she did the motions over and over. She'd take a handful of lollipops and whiz them past my head, cackling when she'd notice me duck a little. "Don't worry. You'll only get one upside the head if you try to hit on Rhett."

"Stop it, Fern." Rhett's body tensed, his knuckles white as he gripped the wheel. "I'm only doing this as a favor to my aunt."

"Mmhhmm. Just smile for the paper when we get up here." She tapped me on the shoulder. "Can I have my glasses back?"

I pulled them off of my face and handed them back to her, only to have her throw them on the floorboard, where I had to pick them up.

"Smile!" I heard someone yell when my head was between my legs. When I jerked up with the sunglasses in my hand, I realized Fern had thrown the glasses on the floor so whoever was taking a photo of her and Rhett didn't get me in the picture.

I cocked a brow and glanced back at her. She wore what we called in Kentucky a shit-eatin' grin. Forgive my language, but that's what it was.

Little did she know just who was in the car with her.

My name was Violet Rhinehammer, and I was going to show Holiday Junction just who had landed in their town, um Village.

A name they'd never forget.

CHAPTER EIGHT

There was literally nothing I could do.

Literally.

Rhett knew it too. Underneath his mirrored sunglasses, I knew he was side glancing my way, because every time I impatiently drummed my fingers on the door, he'd smirk.

Adding to it, the toe of Miss Fancy Pants's heeled shoe kept digging into the back of my arm. When I'd glance back, she'd murmur an apology under her smile.

"Why couldn't we have that official?" I pointed to the convertible in front of us, where there was a dog hanging out the window.

"That's the most important official in Holiday Junction. I'm second." Fern's toe dug into my arm.

Instead of giving her the satisfaction of me showing any sort of grimace, I slowly scooted closer to the car door. It would be obvious if she toed me again that it was deliberate.

"Who is he?" I wanted to know who had the cute dog. That's the kind of person I wanted to hang out with while I was in this crazy Village.

When we rounded the corner, I got a good look at the cute dog. Fern threw out two handfuls of candy, one for each side.

The smile grew on my face when the little black ears popped out of the window. The children along the parade route went crazy, and when the dog turned its little black head, I noticed the white upside-down wishbone markings that started between the pup's eyes and along each side of its nose.

"Boston terrier?" I questioned with glee. "I have to know who that is in front of us."

"Miss Paisley. She's the Village mayor, and she's a—" Fern started to tell me, but Rhett interrupted her.

"We will introduce you when we get to your destination, which is where the parade route ends." Rhett's words made Fern chuckle.

"What? Is Miss Paisley not a good mayor?" I couldn't help but notice there was some sort of secret between them.

"Everyone loves Miss Paisley. In fact, she's never ever had an opponent during the elections," Rhett said, getting my curiosity up.

"It sounds like Miss Paisley is someone I need to interview while I'm here." I wasn't going to tell them, but I was going to get an interview with the mayor and let her know just how messed up this entire investigation had been going.

I was sure Miss Paisley had no idea the officials had been granted the day off when they should've been called back in because there was a dead body.

I'd spent the rest of the three-mile-per-hour drive down what appeared to be the main street of Holiday Junction thinking about what I was going to say to Mayor Paisley.

The houses had gotten much bigger and stood tall, brick mansions with elaborate fences around them, and I'd guessed they all had nice front yards due to how far the houses were set back.

Holiday Junction was definitely a place that had money, unlike my hometown. The houses melted into the center of Village, where various small shops were next to each other and looked to be interesting. For a second I made a plan to visit a couple of them, but I realized quickly I wasn't going to be here long and put the little shopping adventure out of my head.

The parade route seemed to have stopped at the end of the heart of the Village, and Rhett pulled the car over.

"Move it." Fern had already tried to climb over me to get out.

Pftt, pftt. I spit her tulle out of my mouth and tried to get it out of my face so I could jump out and see the mayor.

"I'm trying," I told her and opened the door to get out. "But you aren't giving me any time."

"I don't have time. This is a major deal, and I've got to go sign some autographs." She adjusted her dress once she got her footing on the sidewalk. When she moved away, the mayor's car was empty.

"Great." I groaned and wondered just how I was going to get in front of the mayor.

The parade continued past us. I could tell by the lineup the mayor was the head of the parade, followed up by Fern, so Fern was well beloved in Holiday Junction.

I stood on the sidewalk, waiting for Rhett to tell me how to get to the hotel.

"Neat, huh." He walked around the convertible and watched the amazing floats pass by. He pointed to the men and women walking in front of the bagpipe band. "That's the Holiday Junction parade committee."

"Y'all have your own parade committee?" I asked and snorted then saw a rooster trotting in front of them. "Someone lost their rooster."

"That's Dave." Rhett smiled. "He's head of the parade security."

"You're joking, right?" It was hard for me to keep my jaw in place as it dropped in disbelief.

"Nope. Dave keeps everyone in line."

The rooster did seem to know what it was doing with its head held high as the committee walked behind him.

"The parade ends with a full day of shamrock fun. Tomorrow is the greening of the Village fountain, which is out in our big park. There's even a small lake there where you can take a pedal boat out." He was talking over the bagpipes as they passed. It was hard to hear him, so we stood there for a minute as the young Celtic dancers did their dance.

"Wow. Those are gorgeous dresses." It was hard to not compliment the dancers' outfits. "I love the huge four-leaf clover on the front."

"Each dress is custom printed, cut, and sewn just for the dancers. That's her over there." He pointed across the street to one of the older dancers. "Leni. She's our local tailor, so she takes her work seriously for the festivals."

"Festivals?" I asked, noticing the woman he'd pointed to was having a heated discussion with another dancer before she gave her a little shove.

"This is just St. Patrick's Day. We have festivals for all the holidays." He nudged me. "I told you that you were going to like it here."

"Fat chance," I told him and stood there watching the large float pass by.

There was no denying the work the organizers of each float had put into their float. All of them had either a skirt of green material wrapped around the outer portion or some sort of crepe paper. One of them was built in the shape of an old Viking ship with cutouts of leprechaun faces, horseshoes, and the Irish flag along the sides of it.

"There's a lot of floats." When I looked down the street, there wasn't a visible end to the parade in sight.

"Yes. Each shop has their own float." He pointed to the next float, where men in kilts and leprechaun hats were singing. "That's the local band, which does perform at the Jubilee Inn." He pointed behind us.

The building was five stories tall with several small balconies across each floor. Some had people standing on the balconies, watching the parade.

"I have a room there?" I asked, digging into my purse for the voucher.

"Yep. I'm not sure how they pulled it off because most of the time the rooms are booked during the holidays, but maybe they had a room for one." He shrugged. "Let's get you inside."

I wasn't sure what it was before it was an inn, but the Jubilee Inn was very cute. The inside was more of an open-type setting, with a lounging area you had to walk through to make it to the back wall. There, a woman was waiting behind a counter.

"Hey there, Rhett." She greeted him by name, which was very comforting to me because where I was from, everyone knew everyone by name.

"This is Violet Rhinehammer." Rhett introduced me to Kristine Whitlock. We shook hands. "She's a big-time reporter. And she's going to be staying here while the"—he leaned over the desk—"crime scene is cleared, and, well, she wants to interview Miss Paisley. I told Ms. Rhinehammer you could facilitate that for us since, well, this is Miss Paisley's residence."

"Mayor Paisley?" An odd look glazed over Kristine's face.

Kristine appeared to be in her sixties with her salt-and-pepper hair. She had a few wrinkles on her forehead and long smile lines that stayed etched on her face after she stopped smiling.

"Yes, ma'am. The one and only mayor. You see, Ms. Rhinehammer here has a problem with the officers taking off today for the parade."

I interrupted him.

"I feel like it needs to be brought to the mayor's attention how no one seemed to worry about Jay Mann's murder. And trust me, it was a murder. I saw him with my own two eyes." I closed my eyes as a shiver rolled up my spine from the memory.

"I see." Kristine finally saw how important it was to me, even though Rhett had seemed to be poking fun at me. "Yes. I think I can arrange it."

"Say around 7 p.m.?" I wanted to make sure I had time to prepare, and that meant getting all the information I could about Holiday Junction's police department as well as finding out anything I could on Jay.

"That's the mayor's dinnertime." Kristine's brows furrowed. "And she does love her dinner."

"I think it's perfect. Where I come from, Normal, Kentucky—" The way she looked at me was the look I always received when I told people I was from Kentucky. They either wanted to know if we all drank bourbon, just how fast were the horses, or if we wore shoes.

Kristine seemed to be thinking the latter as I watched her eyes swoop down to my feet.

"We love to have little chitchats, and eating food is a great time to incorporate those conversations." I watched as Kristine and Rhett both shrugged to each other at my suggestion.

"I guess, but you better be prepared, because she's vivacious when it comes to her food," Kristine said.

"And the well-being of the Village," Rhett followed up.

"Good. Then I have no reason not to think that Mayor Paisley and I will see eye to eye." I took the room key off the counter. "See, I've been here under a couple of hours, and I am already going to be making lemonade out of lemons." I turned but quickly turned back. The two of them jumped to attention as if I'd walked back into a private conversation.

"Hmmm," I sighed so they knew I knew that they were being secretive. I let it go. "Do you happen to have a phone charger I can buy or borrow?"

"We have those in the rooms for our guests. If you need to purchase one, you can take a right out of the inn, and just a couple of blocks next to Brewing Beans is the Jovial General Store."

"Brewing Beans? Is that a place to get coffee?" I asked. "I love a good cup of coffee."

"Yes, and it's good, too, but I'm sure the line is long today because of all the festivities. But it's worth the wait." Kristine's face told me it was the place to go.

"Thank you." I smiled on my way up to my room because seeing the sunny side of things always put a little giddyup in my steps.

CHAPTER NINE

I mmediately I put my phone on the charger to get it good and juiced up so I could get in touch with Richard and schedule another live for the station. It was a surefire way for me to slip right on into the open broadcaster position I was destined for.

It felt so good knowing exactly what my life was going to look like. It was a sad and unfortunate event about poor Jay Mann, and, well, if it weren't for his untimely death, I mightn't've gotten the job. But I was sure it was in the bag now.

"There." I had found the phone charger on the bedside table, just like Kristine had mentioned, and I sat down just to take a load off my feet.

They were killing me, but there was little time to really stop and rest. I couldn't change my shoes because they were on the airplane and Chief Strickland hadn't released anyone's luggage.

"Something told me to wear sensible shoes," I said to myself. I took off the pumps I wore because I hadn't wanted Richard Stone, or whoever was picking me up at the airport to take me to the interview, to see me in tennis shoes.

I rubbed my feet and closed my eyes to think about the beach a few blocks from here and how nice it would feel to put my toes in the sand. Heck, it would be nice to bury my head there too.

I looked at my phone after it beeped a few text messages, one after the other. I wasn't sure if I wanted to look at them or not. I couldn't bear to know who in Normal saw how disheveled I looked in the national headlines.

I was a glutton for punishment, so I went against my better judgement and reached for the phone.

"It won't hurt to scroll through." I scooted down the edge of the bed to get closer to the bedside table so the charger wouldn't get pulled out of my phone.

I snorted a laugh when I noticed the texts were from people I tried to stay away from. Unfortunately, it was those people that would probably help me out the most.

Then I came up to a text message from Maybelline West. She had moved to my hometown without a penny to her name, and she'd made a big life for herself.

Sorta the same situation I was going to be in. Sorta. Only her past was that she had to move because she was broke. Still, we both moved somewhere where we knew no one. Though I wasn't to my final destination yet, she just might be someone to help me out of this little pickle because she did know a few things about snooping around to get some answers.

I hit the message and didn't read it. I clicked on her name and hit the call button.

"Hello?" I could tell by the way Mae answered the phone that she was a little taken aback by my call.

"Hi, Mae." I cleared my throat. "I-I-I," I stammered.

"You're in a little situation, aren't you?" she asked. "You need some help? I'm here to help."

"I know that you and I did some snooping around a few times during my time at the *Normal Gazette* and Channel Two." I didn't have to remind her how we'd gotten keys to the city and all that.

Both of us were good at what we did. There could've been a little healthy competition between the two of us, but it was all in fun.

"Violet, you don't need to say anything to me. We are friends, no matter how much we disagreed in the past, and there's nothing I'd love to see more than for you to succeed in whatever that may be. How can I help you?"

"I'm stuck here in St. Patrick's Day hell, literally. The entire Village is crazy for this holiday, and everywhere I turn, there's green, green, and greener." I smiled when I heard Mae snickering on the other end of the phone as I told my crazy story, including how I'd gotten stuck in the middle of the parade with Miss Holiday Junction sticking the heel of her shoe in my side.

"Rhett, huh?" There was a tickle of tease in Mae's voice.

"He's a nice guy, and in a different life, maybe we'd date. But he is the security guard at the airport." I proceeded to tell her how his uncle was the police chief and how the other officers were off for the holiday. "As much as I hate to admit it, this could actually seal the deal for the job if I could solve it while the airplane is grounded."

"It's part of a small Village." Mae reminded me of just how backwards Normal could be sometimes too. "You just have to take matters into your own hands."

"How do I do that?" I asked her.

"First off, you need to find out everything you can about the victim. Where they are from. If they are married. Stores he liked to frequent. Family member, anything." I tried to write everything she was saying but Mae West talked so fast. "Once you get that information, find their phone numbers, emails anything to get in touch with them. Then you ask around as you call the stores, get food, call his local newspaper, or the paper boy, about the victim and what type of person he was. Then you just might have to ask some basic questions, like did he have any enemies or make someone mad. Make a list."

I reached into my purse and took out the notepad to write down all the things Mae was saying, even though I knew most of this stuff as a journalist. It was good to hear it again because being in the thick of a murder and finding the body put me in a much different headspace than doing a story where I was far removed from it.

"If you can get your hands on a police scanner, that'd be great too."

Mae started to jog my memory on all the things I knew to do, and it took me right back to college, to my Journalism 101 class. "You know all this stuff. I think you are just nervous and grabbing at straws to get you to the job interview. If you take a moment to put down some thoughts on paper, one thing at a time, and really keep your ears open, you'll get some clues that'll help you solve the murder."

"It's funny how when I lived in Normal, you were doing this to solve the murder while I was doing this to chase the story. It's much different solving than gathering facts to type up." I laughed, realizing just how much I'd judged Mae for getting up in everyone's business.

"At the end of the day, I think both of us were trying to do better for our community. While you're in Holiday Junction, you're going to have to think of it as your community for right now. You'll get the story. I don't know if you'll be able to solve the murder, but I do know you are smart. Any clues you do gather will help the police so they don't have to chase after the clues, which will get them closer to solving the murder and you closer to your dream job."

"Thank you, Mae." My heart tugged as I thought about how she and I could've joined forces much more while I lived in Normal to solve all the crimes together. But it hadn't been the right timing for either of us. "This will make me a better journalist for sure."

"You're already a great one." Mae gave me the vote of confidence I needed to get out there and get my ear to the ground. "Call me if you need to bounce any ideas or anything you hear off me."

"Will do." We said our goodbyes.

While I let my phone charge up even more, I went into the bathroom and wiped off the makeup from underneath my eyes, ran my fingers through my hair, and retrieved the lipstick from my purse. I was at least a little more presentable than before and not so scary. Granted, if Holiday Junction had been celebrating Halloween, I would've fit right in as a zombie news reporter.

I grabbed my notebook and my phone, threw both in my bag, and set out into the streets and Shamrock Festival, where I was determined to get some clues.

"Violet!" I heard Rhett's familiar voice calling to me.

I ignored him by pretending I couldn't hear over the crowd. I slowly turned my head in the opposite direction on purpose.

"Violet Rhinehammer! Violet!" His voice got so loud on the last call of my name. I shifted my body so my back was to him.

"Give her a little nip!" I heard Rhett call out to the barista as he made his way down the counter.

"No, you will not!" I jerked around.

"Ha! I knew you could hear me. Were you ignoring me on purpose, Ms. Rhinehammer?" Rhett sidled up next to me.

"Don't you dare put anything but black coffee in that cup," I warned the barista.

"They don't have liquor here." Rhett leaned his hip on the counter. He smelled of beer. "I knew it would get your uptight attention." He laughed when I picked up the coffee. He threw down a few dollars. "On me."

"I can pay my own way, thank you." I dug down into my purse.

"No. Keep your money. It's the least I can do to tell you how sorry I am for Fern. She can be a little over the top sometimes. No one in the Village has come close to giving her any competition until you." Rhett caught me off guard.

"Excuse me?" I asked before I could get my money out. The barista took Rhett's, and he took me by the elbow to lead me out into the street.

He dropped his hand and lifted his chin up to the sky. He sucked in a deep breath and let out a long sigh. He pointed left.

"This way to the Shamrock Festival Stein Competition." Vigorously, he rubbed his hands together. "You can be my partner."

"Shamrock Festival Stein Competition?" I felt an overwhelming sensation of intuition telling me *no way, no how, hell no* was I going to do any sort of competition.

"Everyone keeps asking me who the new girl is and why was she in my car with Fern. Fern doesn't like it one bit, and, well, she's not only Miss Holiday Junction. She's also in the five-time Shamrock

Festival Stein Competition champ group." He looked down at me and grinned. "You're stuck here for at least a couple of days. Enjoy the Shamrock Festival. You might end up liking it and come back next year."

"This time next year I'll be doing a huge interview like—" I searched my brain. "You name the movie star, and I'll prove to you that I'll be doing that this time next year."

I loved a good challenge.

"Then you will look back fondly on your time here and maybe one day fly through to where you can say that you were the talent we needed on my team to bring down the five-time champs in the Shamrock Festival Stein Competition." He smirked. "Your name will be engraved on the big stein forever."

"Oh, I do like that." My shoulders lowered. "Fine. What do I do?"

"Come on." Rhett grabbed my hand and wove us in and out of the crowd in the street and down a little farther, where they'd marked off twenty feet.

"Isn't this competition more for a German festival?" I asked when I noticed there were four teams with a set of five in the group.

They stood in front of a table with five steins filled to the brim with golden, bubbly beer.

"Maybe." His right shoulder lifted, as did his lip as though he didn't have a care in the world. "But it's a competition we do here for the Shamrock Festival, and we drink on this day. Now Mother's Day is around the corner, and there's zero drinking on that day." He lifted his hand in a gesture of zero.

Fern tossed her hair, catching my peripheral vision. I was sure she'd done it on purpose, because when I looked her way, her face wore a vengeful scowl before she leaned into the ear of a burly man wearing plaid, who had shifted his gaze from the ground over to me.

He smirked.

She sashayed her way over to my new group.

"I see you've been recruited. Didn't he tell you how they've never won?" She cackled. "Or are you just the new tourist flavor of the week?"

She tapped her temples. "I don't recall him ever bragging about a girl from Kentucky."

"I'm a woman, and I'm not a tourist, nor do I have any interest in Rhett Strickland." I took a big swig of my hot coffee.

Just the sight of her looking at my hot coffee made my body temperature rise, and I had a picture of me being the one on this team to clinch the win, holding up that big—and what looked to be plastic—stein trophy with my name on it up in the air as she ran off crying.

"And we are going to win." I dropped my coffee in the trash can as if I were doing that whole drop-the-mic impression.

"I'd be worried if I were you." She winked and went back to join her group. They all turned and laughed before they huddled together.

"Everyone, this is Violet Rhinehammer, and she's going to be our fifth." Rhett's announcement to the group sure didn't sit well. They talked among themselves as if I weren't there.

"Really, Rhett?" The other woman besides me on the team peered over top of her eyeglasses. "She was just drinking coffee."

"At least let us know she does drink beer." The skinniest man in the group eyed me up and down.

"Or is even legal to drink." The other, heavyset guy put in his comment.

"Come on, guys. Give her a chance." Rhett put his arm around my shoulders. "Right, Violet?" He gave a hard nod and looked at me with a smile. It faded. "You do drink, right?"

"Yeah, sure." I lied because I just wanted to prove Fern and now them wrong about me. "Let's do this!"

"That's what I'm talking about." Rhett put his hand in the middle of our little circle. "On the count of three, we do 'shamrock.'"

All of our hands were one on top of the other.

"One"—our hands started to bounce to Rhett's count—"two, three!" We flung our hands high above our heads. "Shamrock!" we all yelled.

For someone who had no idea what this competition was about and also who rarely drank, I did really well on my first go at it. Let me be clear that I had no idea of the rules, and if I'd known that I had to run the distance to the other table at the far end of the course with the full stein of beer with little to none sloshing out, only to down the entire thing before I picked up another stein, only to go back to where I'd started, I'd not have said yes to Rhett.

Whichever team had just one member standing was the winner, and when it got down to me and Fern, my ignorance of not only this competition but of drinking was what carried me that far.

While my teammates were taking their turn, I'd decided to focus on Fern's team and take my mind off the fact I was about to drink a beer.

Bleh.

"Hurry up and go take off that dress. If you spill beer on it, no more fancy stuff for you," the man in Fern's group told the woman I'd recognized from the parade.

Not the woman who made the dresses, but the woman who had bumped into or stepped on the other. The one who got shoved.

"Don't tell me what I can and can't do." She got right back into his face. "I might be your wife, but I'm my own person, and you can't make me do anything."

"It's my money, and you spend every dime!" He got up in her face with his chest popped out.

"Your turn!" Fern had noticed the argument between the man and wife. She put her hand on the man.

He gave one more glare to his wife before he grabbed a beer stein off the tray and headed to the other side of the maze, where their other teammates were cheering him on.

"What?" Fern snarled.

"You're gonna get fat." I knew that'd get her attention.

"I can exercise." She grabbed the stein before I could even get mine, and she darted off.

After I'd gone twice around the maze, I ignored how Holiday Junction was spinning around me and held onto the image of me holding that plastic trophy above my head as my team chanted my name.

"Mmmmhhhh awwww." Fern wiped her mouth with her forearm after she'd downed the next stein on the third round.

"All of those calories. I don't care," I lied, trying to gulp back the beer. "And where I'm from—" I started to say.

"We know. You're from Kentucky." She belched the last bit as we stumbled along the course to make it to the finish line, where we would have one last beer.

"Yeah, and we drink real moonshine. Not that fake stuff. The real deal. So this beer is nothing to me." I went to grab the last stein and down it, but as luck would have it, Fern threw her hands up in the air.

"We have a new champion!" I heard the voice scream out before Rhett and the members of our team grabbed me up and threw me in the air.

"I told you I was somebody." My words slurred, and I pumped my fists in the air.

It was a moment I was sure I'd never forget if I could only remember all of it, but all I heard after Rhett took the trophy was how I was going to be late for my dinner with the mayor.

"But I didn't even get to investigate the police force," I said as I stumbled along the street on the way back to Junction Inn. The crowd of onlookers at the competition had joined us on our victory walk, clapping the entire time.

I pulled the black silk square from my pocket and whirled it in the air.

"And I didn't get to take this to the morgue!" My head was flung back like I had no muscles. "Rhett, what am I going to do?"

"You're going to go to bed, and the mayor will have to wait until the morning." It was the last thing I remembered.

CHAPTER TEN

The knock at the door of my room brought me to life. I sat on the bed, wondering how on earth I'd gotten there, then I remembered.

"Rhett," I seethed. I tumbled out of bed and tried to get my footing before I went to the door and swung it open. "Rhett, you did this."

"Good morning." Kristine Whitlock stood on the other side with a tray. The little black-and-white Boston terrier was at her side.

"I thought you were Rhett." I opened the door wide for her to enter. "I was going to give him a piece of my mind." I bent down and patted the dog.

Her lips twitched as though she was trying to contain the smile growing.

"I thought you could use this." She put the tray on the small table next to the double doors that led out to the balcony that jutted out over the main street.

There was a covered plate along with a small bottle of headache medication.

"I also thought you might need to take a couple of these. If you don't have a headache now, you will." She picked up the bottle and shook it. "You've made quite the impression around here. I don't ever recall another tourist becoming so well-known in just a few hours. Everyone is talking about Jay Mann being found." She pulled the blinds on the double door open.

The sun popped out to show the glorious weather for today.

"I'm not a tourist." I stood up and walked over to the king-sized four-poster bed with a canopy. It had a thin ceiling curtain that was white and sheer and fell around the bed, making it look like a little princess bed.

I loved it.

"The police let out his name?" Now I knew everyone all over the world would know the story before I could get a jump on it.

"Yes. He will be missed." Kristine put her hands to her heart.

"Wait. You knew him?" I questioned and grabbed my notebook off the small desk next to the double doors where I could do some work if I needed to over the next few hours. I hoped that was all the time the police needed before they let us leave.

"Jay was a very prominent citizen here, and I bet Melissa is beside herself. She and Jay have a granddaughter who needs a kidney transplant. Something about a rare condition. From what I understand, Jay and Melissa have been traveling back and forth to their daughter's home. That's why he was on the airplane, coming home."

"Where's the daughter live?" I asked and wondered if I could make it there to talk to her.

"An airplane ride away." She had no idea. "Jay was coming back home for the festival since he was being honored as a past Hibernians Grand Marshal today. Something they do every year during the Shamrock Festival."

She lifted the lid off of the plate. The smell of the eggs, bacon, and toast fluttered throughout the room.

"Anyways, the Manns drive two hours to Banchester, where they catch an airplane to go to their daughter. From what I understand, he was on his way back when he was killed."

"His wife was not with him?" I asked.

"No, but I also heard she, Sandra, and the granddaughter are on their way back now in light of what happened." Kristine's lips twitched back and forth. "I can't remember the name of their grandchild for the life of me. I know it too. Kristine talked about it so much at the Ladies of the Hibernian Society."

I recognized the name Banchester since it was the only stop on my flight where I had to disembark and grab another airplane to my final destination.

"Hibernian Society?" I questioned.

"Oh yeah. It's a big deal in Holiday. Really it's more for our Irish citizens, but I'm not Irish, and they needed members. Jay and Melissa, or maybe just Melissa, have some Irish descent in their family, so they were big contributors to the society."

"I wonder if he was murdered by someone in the society?" My little journalist mind came to life, forgetting all about the hangover.

Give me a good lead, or in this case possible lead, for a great story, and all the adrenaline made all the aches and pains go away. My blood was pumping.

"I don't think so." Kristine shook her head.

"Cute pup." I changed the subject because I could tell by the way she was acting that she didn't even think it possible.

As a journalist, I knew anything was possible, even the unthinkable.

"I saw him in the parade with the mayor." I referred to the dog and walked over to pick up the piece of toast. I needed carbs to soak up the beer still left in my system.

"Her. She's a her," Kristine corrected me.

"I should've known because you are so cute." I talked baby talk to the pup. "What's your name?" I bent down and looked at her little pink collar with the metal tag. "Paisley. Just like your mayor. How cute."

"This is Miss Paisley," Kristine said.

"I see that." I scratched her head before I took the mug of coffee from the tray. "Must be a popular name because of the mayor."

I snickered before I took a sip of coffee.

"No. This is Mayor Paisley." She referred to the dog.

I spit my coffee out of my mouth, showering Kristine's shirt.

"I'm so sorry." I put the mug down and tried to help wipe her down. "I am not generally like this, but I thought you said this dog was the mayor."

"She is." Kristine ran her hands down her shirt. "She has been our elected mayor for seven years now."

"You know what?" I shook my head and walked over to my phone. "I'm thinking there's a rental car place here, and I can just drive across the country to California."

"You're not crazy. She's our mayor."

"How is that possible?" This was almost as intriguing as why someone would kill Jay Mann.

"The Village has never had a human mayor. Each election cycle, people from around the world cast their votes to elect a canine one. It's mostly just fun and a distraction from the tension of human politics, but each voter pays one dollar per vote, and proceeds go to the Holiday Historical Society. This year, they raised nearly twenty-three thousand dollars."

"What?" Now this might be a story that'd go viral over the AP.

Kristine laughed.

"Okay, I have to know what Mayor Paisley's duties are."

"They include sitting on the front porch of the inn, taking pictures with visitors, and chewing on bones, as well as wearing her cute little outfits." Kristine ran her hand down Mayor Paisley. "She's a doll, and she's all mine."

Suddenly I felt so dumb as I recalled how I'd acted yesterday, demanding to see the mayor. Little did I realize how Rhett had played me like a fiddle and I fell for it.

"Anyways, there's been another murder." Kristine's eyes shifted to my bedside table, where I'd put the silk pocket scarf that'd fallen off of Jay's body.

"Another one?" *Was this one related to Jay's?* How odd was this. My mind was racing so much that I hadn't noticed Kristine had moved over to the table, where she picked up the pocket scarf.

"Where did you get this?" she asked in a demanding voice. "Answer me now, or I'm calling Chief Strickland."

"It fell off of Jay Mann's body when the coroner took him out of the airport. I'm going to go to the morgue today and return it."

"Are you sure?" Kristine dropped it back on the side table. "Because Rosey Hume was found this morning in the Holiday Park fountain with the exact same pocket square stuffed in her mouth and what they think was a knife wound."

CHAPTER ELEVEN

I couldn't get Kristine and Mayor Paisley out of my room fast enough. Another person with the same pocket square was found dead, and both lived here in Holiday Junction. This story was greater than we'd initially imagined.

Holiday Junction was the big clue to me due to the fact that two of its citizens were murdered. There was no way that the two deaths weren't related in some fashion, and the killer on the airplane had to have been from Holiday Junction.

Was the killer right under my nose? Had I passed the killer on the street yesterday?

Had Jay Mann and Rosey Hume known each other and known something that made someone want to silence them forever?

I quickly got cleaned up and took the headache medication just in case, before I threw on some sunglasses to cover my puffy eyes and bolted out the door.

"Richard, it's Violet." I spoke in a serious tone to his voicemail. "I know you want me to report on the murder, but you aren't going to believe this. There are two murders, and I think we've got a real story here. I'm still not sure when the local yahoo police is going to let us take off, but in the meantime, there's no reason I can't snoop around."

I pinched a grin when passing another guest at the inn as I took the steps to the lobby.

"Call me back." I clicked the phone off and dropped my phone back in my purse.

"Where you off to?" Kristine called from behind the counter.

"Fountain?" I questioned, throwing my finger up in the air and pointing right and then left, giving her the answer to her question while asking for directions.

"Right. You can't miss it. Just keep walking and you'll run right smack dab into it," she said, her voice growing in volume as I pushed open the doors of the Jubilee Inn and walked right into a photo shoot with Mayor Paisley and a line of tourists.

Everyone looked like they'd walked through green slime from their head-to-toe attire. Even Mayor Paisley had on a shamrock dress.

Kristine was right. The fountain and the park was at the very end of Main Street. It was as far as you could go.

From a distance I noticed there was police tape around the large four-tiered concrete fountain. The closer I got, the faster I walked and maneuvered my way through the crowd.

When I got a good luck at the fountain I figured it to be about twelve feet wide and about a two-feet-deep pool where there were four ceramic swans with water flowing out of their mouths. There was a top on the fountain that was a large ceramic watering can ever so slightly tipped over, with water pouring out of it as well.

As I got even closer, I noticed there were four large sidewalks going away from the fountain. When I got to the sign I noticed it where each sidewalk would lead.

The south would take me to the seaside, the north would take me back toward the mountains, the east towards Village, and the west to the countryside. Too bad there wasn't going to be enough time to explore them all or even go to the beach, but where I was going, I would live by the beach.

The park was very large and grassy. Just like Rhett had mentioned, there was a small lake type body of water with pedal boats all tied up to a wooden dock.

There were benches along the sidewalks for people to sit, but other than that, it didn't have anything but grass. There was a large white structure with marble pillars and marble blocks that appeared to be seating in the grassy area in front. The structure looked like it was some sort of stage that was home to the Village Players, a local theater group.

After looking around to get a good sense of where I was, I turned around and recognized Chief Strickland and the man who had put Jay in the hearse where near the fountain. I headed that way.

"I can't believe it. Poor Rosey." There was some murmuring filtering through the few people I wiggled my way past so I could get up to the front. All of them wore green suits with white sashes with the words "Hibernian Society" glittering in gold.

"Why on earth was she trying to turn the fountain green when she knew it was part of the ceremony?"

"Rosey?" I gasped, putting my hand over my mouth. "That's awful."

"Two Hibernians in twenty-four hours." The woman tsked. "Do you think we are in danger? Are they plucking us off one at a time?"

"Rosey and Jay were Hibernians?" I wanted to be sure I heard everything correctly so when I reported it back to Richard, I had all the facts.

"Are you that reporter from the airport?" Another lady in the group noticed me. "You are, but you don't have all that crazy makeup on your face."

"It had been a long day and—" I found myself explaining my disheveled appearance from yesterday. "Yes." I decided not to even worry about it. What mattered was right now and these facts I was collecting. "Do you think you're in danger?"

"The members of the Hibernians never get along with each other. How could they? They don't even like each other." She rolled her eyes. "If Jay Mann wasn't dead, I'd have pegged him to have killed Rosey. They fought at the last meeting about who was going to turn the fountain green, and, well, as you can see, she was going to do it, but someone stopped her."

"What is the protocol for turning the fountain green?" It was something I could've easily looked up on my phone, but hearing from someone who'd seen it firsthand was much better for the reporting piece.

I took my notepad out of my purse and started to write down word for word what she was telling me.

"The Hibernians pick a child from the community to come to the ceremony, which better still be happening today." She shifted her weight and looked at her friend. They both nodded. "Just like Rosey to make it all about her."

There was no love lost between Rosey and this group of citizens.

"That doesn't matter now." The woman turned back to finish telling me about the fountain. "The child will pick up that small green watering can you see over there." She pointed, and my eyes followed but fell on Chief Strickland.

He was staring back at me. I acted like I didn't see him by looking back at my notebook. The woman continued.

"After some words are read, the chosen child will pick up the can and pour in the dye. Which is environmentally friendly. You can write that down." Her lips pressed together, and her eyes grew. Her expression told me she wanted the little fact on paper.

I scribbled it down, satisfying her so she would continue.

"It only takes a few seconds for the dye to turn all the water green. It lasts about three days, long enough until the end of the festival." She threw her hand in the air. "Hey there!" She hurried off with the other ladies following her.

"Can I get your name?" I called after her, but she didn't hear me. Instead of chasing her down, I decided I needed to go see exactly what Chief Strickland was thinking.

"I see you've made some friends with some of the locals." He didn't move his head as his eyes shifted to the right, looking in the direction of the woman who'd just given me the lowdown on the fountain. His eyes moved in a line to look at me. "I'm sure they have already figured out who the killer is since they know all the gossip."

"Matthew, there's bloodstains on the edge of the fountain, so she was killed here. Then a body must have been dragged into the water. I'd say we're looking for a knife with a long, thin blade."

"Can I get your name?" I asked the man, with my pen at the ready.

"Excuse us." Matthew stepped in between me and the coroner.

"I can find out his name. And you should just tell me. Besides, I have some information that might interest you and him." I opened my purse and took out the pocket square.

Both men's jaws dropped.

"Curtis Robinson." He stuck out his hand. "Where did you get that?"

"I was standing outside the airport when you pushed the gurney to the hearse, and this dropped off of Jay Mann's body." Leaning over to see around them, I saw the tips of Rosey Hume's shoes sticking up out of the water in the middle of the fountain. Everything else but the tip of her nose was submerged, and where her mouth was located, there was a piece of cloth floating in place.

"Ms. Rhinehammer was the passenger who found Jay on the airplane." Chief Strickland introduced us in his way. "I looked you up. From what I gathered from Sheriff Hemmer."

"You called Sheriff Hemmer?" I put my journalist poker face on, which I felt was pretty good when I couldn't help but wonder what on earth Al Hemmer had told him. "And?"

"He said you were a true journalist and you had a knack for using your skills to aid in a few of his cases in Normal, Kentucky." Chief Strickland stared at me.

"Ahem." I cleared my throat and tugged on the hem of my shirt. "He's right. I didn't leave those skills back in Normal. I'm willing to offer my services to you, Matthew."

He jerked his head as if I had the gall to call him by his name. His eyes narrowed.

"I can call you Matthew, right? I mean if we are going to be working together." I ignored Curtis when I saw him smirking. "It seems to me that these two crimes are related. The victims are both from Holiday

Junction, both were in the Hibernian Society. It seems like there's a killer among us."

"Just how do you explain Jay being murdered on an airplane?" he questioned with a little bit of a grin as if he were testing me in hopes I'd fail.

"Obviously someone wanted him dead, and they had to be on the airplane. So do you have the passenger list?" I asked.

The sound of someone crying made me look. There was a woman near the edge of the park, talking with a Holiday Junction officer. He appeared to be questioning her. She had a dog on a leash.

"We do have the passenger list, and I've split it up among my officers to make sure we get all of their statements, taking their personal information, and letting them leave. We can't keep them here forever." Matthew's wide stance, hand on his utility belt, and stiff posture gave me the vibe he wasn't quite sure of me yet.

"Great! Then I'm sure you can get all this figured out on your own, because I've got to get to California. I'm already late for a big interview, and, well, I'm not qualified to do any sort of police work." I couldn't wait to get back to the Jubilee Inn so I could check out and get back to the airport. "If you'll excuse me."

"Hold up!" Matthew stopped me. "We are only on the B's, and you are an R for Rhinehammer, so we won't be getting to your part of the alphabet for, I'd say, forty-eight hours."

"Are you holding me against my will?" I hated always having my name be at practically the end of the alphabet. Even in school it sucked.

"I'm sorry, Ms. Rhinehammer. You were so eager to give your two cents and running around trying to get some sort of footage. I called that fancy station out in California, and they told me you didn't have a job but that interview. And, well, I guess I could hold you longer and make you even later." He had something up his sleeve.

"You can't do that." I jerked back and noticed a few more people being interviewed by the officers.

"If Sheriff Hemmer didn't give you such a glowing recommendation on how great you are at snooping, then I might've let you leave, but the fact you found the victim and you have the pocket square leaves me to think you might've taken the pocket square when you two could've argued on the airplane."

"Did someone say I was arguing with someone on the airplane?" My jaw dropped at the lie.

"I don't know. I've not gotten everyone's statement. You aren't cleared to leave, so why not just help out with that special nosy technique you have?" He had me. He knew it, and I knew it.

"My two cents is that they had a possible affair. His wife killed him and then her." I started to throw out ideas.

"Melissa is out of town and should be in before the Greening of the Fountain to accept Jay's award." He let me know she had an alibi.

"What about Rosey's husband? He heard about the affair. Let's face it. The top reasons someone is murdered is love, greed, and/or money." I shrugged.

"I would love to interview Rosey's husband, but we've already talked to him." His head tilted to the right, his ear nearly touching his shoulder as he crossed his arms.

"I'm going to need the passenger list." I knew all my excuses could have a comeback, and there was no way I was going to get to my already-day-late interview for another forty-eight hours. I might'swell make good use of my time.

"No problem." He whistled really loudly, catching the attention of someone I couldn't see due to the bright sunshine.

As the figure came into focus, I knew it was Rhett.

"Rhett is going to take you down to the station this afternoon, and you can look over some files. I normally wouldn't do this, but when Sheriff Hemmer gave you a glowing recommendation, I decided to use you while you are here." I heard him, but all I could think about was Al Hemmer and how I couldn't wait to give him a piece of my mind.

"Why is she still dressed in her green parade dress?" Curtis interrupted us and made a really good observation. Someone from the coroner's office had wheeled the cart to the fountain and had gotten in to retrieve the body.

"She'd been in the parade, so maybe she still had the dress on."

"The pocket square?" Curtis questioned. "It's the same as the one Violet claims fell off Jay, and I didn't see it on Jay's body when I took him off the airplane."

"Maybe it was in his pocket, and jiggling him down those airplane steps then wheeling him could've possibly wiggled it out of the pocket of his pants? Or maybe when I went in to get his wallet because the pilot asked me to—" I gulped, knowing Jim Dixon was adamant about me getting Jay's identification. He was definitely someone I needed to see.

"What?" Matthew had seen the light bulb in my head click on.

"Jim Dixon. Have you talked to the pilot?" I questioned.

"We let him go because he had to work, but we do have his contact information."

My jaw tensed after I heard this little bit of news.

"I'm going to need that info." There was nothing I could do about Jim now, so I focused on what I could. "That's how I got the square, but I can snoop around to see if anyone has seen these. Who found her?" I asked and slipped the pocket square back into my purse, since I knew they wouldn't use Jay's because I'd put my fingerprints all over it.

"Her." Matthew gave a slight head nod over to the woman still crying.

"And you honestly want me to see what I can find out?" I asked to make sure he wasn't going to cuff me then and there for some unknown reason. "No strings attached. No jail."

"Should I take you to jail?" He got awfully suspicious.

"No," I blurted. "I think it's odd you'd ask for my help."

"According to Sheriff Hemmer, I should use you while you're here if you're still going to insist on doing the story anyways." He made a great point.

"I get to see all the files?" I pointed to Curtis. "Even his files?"

Curtis shuffled his shoes and looked down at the ground.

"Yes. All the files." He made Curtis sigh and me smile.

"And I get to do the lead story with all the information?" I wanted to make sure I got something bigger than just having facts. I wanted the entire story.

"Yes. But I'm asking you to not write all the information until we get someone in custody. We won't talk to any other press." Matthew was being way too nice, but it was fine.

"Good." I turned back and stopped while I watched Curtis go back over to the fountain, where they were retrieving the body. It seemed they'd finished combing it for clues.

My jaw dropped when I recognized the woman.

"What?" Matthew had noticed my change in body language.

"I saw her in the parade yesterday." I gulped and recalled her as the woman who'd not only been shoved by the lady they said made those green dresses, but also as the same lady who'd been on Fern's team.

But who more importantly had argued with her husband.

"You're going to realize ninety percent of the residents were in the parade." He didn't seem that interested in my observation, so I decided I'd just keep my little bit of information to myself and see where it took me before I pointed fingers at her husband.

I glanced back at the woman who'd found Rosey Hume.

"What's her name?" I asked.

"Layla Camsen. Rhett, you want to go with her?" By having Rhett go with me, I knew it was a sign Matthew didn't fully trust me.

That was fine. I'd use the time with Rhett to quiz him on Layla.

"What does Layla do?" I asked Rhett as we took the long way around the fountain to give me time to get a little background information on Layla.

"She owns Holiday Junction Travel Agency. She and her husband, Joaquin. They are longtime residents and pretty well-liked people." He told me enough for me to come up with a couple of questions.

"Hi, Layla, I'm Violet Rhinehammer." I put my hands in my pockets when I noticed she'd given Rhett a glance as if she wanted to see if I was okay to talk to.

He gave a nod and slight smile.

"I know who you are. It's all over the paper this morning." First time

I'd heard that, but I guessed when you get a big story out into the world like Jay's murder on the airplane, before Matthew had shut me down, the word still got out.

Even in Holiday Junction.

"I'm not here as a reporter." So that wasn't entirely true since I'd turn her statement into a piece after we got the killer. "I'm here on behalf of Chief Matthew."

"You think you were in the paper as a reporter?" she asked. "You were in the paper for knocking Fern off from the championship in the Shamrock Festival Stein Competition yesterday."

My eyes blinked a few times as the news settled into my brain before I lowered them.

I gulped, smiled, and laughed.

"How fun." I wrinkled my nose. "Anyways, I know you told the officers about finding Rosey. Can you tell me one more time so I can record it?"

"This is Monty, my dog. He loves to go on his walks here in the park. I knew it was going to be busy this morning, so we came a little earlier because he likes to run off his leash." Her eyes grew when she abruptly stopped talking.

"What?" I asked.

"Well, I guess it doesn't matter anymore, but Rosey was a stickler about leash laws here in Holiday Junction, and she'd tell on you in a minute if you did something wrong. But Monty has a hard time going number two on a leash. Right, Monty?" She looked down at her dog. His tongue was hanging out and his tail wagging, dragging on the grass.

I wrote down word for word what she was saying and found it very interesting that Rosey was what Layla called a stickler.

I wanted to get any and all complaints from the police department. What if she told on someone one too many times?

"What can you tell me about Rosey Hume?" I asked.

"Besides that, she was a very nice person. Though she did like to argue." Layla scoffed. "I bet she's arguing with someone up there." She lifted her brows to the heavens.

Rhett and I looked at each other and smiled, trying not to laugh.

"I understand you don't want to speak ill of the dead, and we aren't asking you to, but we just want the facts. So you are saying you were here earlier than normal. Like what time?" I asked.

"I don't know the time, but I do know it was still dark. So around six thirtyish." She shrugged. "The reason I know is because I heard this squeaking noise like wheels or something. It got Monty's attention, and I got a little scared. It sounded so eerie."

"Where did the sound come from?" I asked.

"Over there." Layla pointed to the woods a little distance from the fountain.

"You were in the woods?" I asked.

"Monty smelled something, so I let him lead me." She jerked her head up to look at me. "Oh my dear, do you think Monty was tracking the killer?" She bent down. "Good boy, Monty. You are so good."

"We don't know that, but maybe." I liked the idea.

"No. We can't say for sure." Rhett put a stop to Layla and me praising Monty. "Don't write that down."

"Fine." My brows furrowed, and I went back to the questions. "You heard a squeak noise, and then you did what?"

"I got out of the woods so we could go home. Monty does like to take a drink out of the fountain, which Rosey would die if she knew it."

"What else can you tell me about her?" I asked.

"Rosey is the secretary of the Hibernians and a long-standing member of the committee, as well as her husband, Zack." Now this was something I could hang my hat on.

"We were told she and her husband did have an argument yesterday at the Shamrock Festival Stein Competition." Again, I saw to it that I spun the words around just a little. "Did you happen to know anything about that?"

"No. I was busy at the booth. My husband and I own the travel agency here. Though I don't put it past them to argue. I heard you found Jay Mann, and if he hadn't been at the airport when he was killed, I'd say it was either Rosey or Zack who killed him."

My ears perked up, and I didn't dare look at Rhett. He was fidgeting. "What do you mean?" I asked and stopped writing to look at her.

"Zack didn't like Rosey being the secretary because she had to work with Jay some. Zack is jealous of Jay. Zack was always saying how Rosey tried to keep up with the same lifestyle as the Manns but they didn't have the Mann money." She laughed. "No one has the Mann money."

She shrugged.

"That said, Zack tried to get Rosey to leave the committee, but there was no way she was going to do that. What on earth would Rosey do with her time? That's when she'd file all those reports on people. She'd hear some gossip then put herself in a situation to see if the gossip was real. If say, for instance, someone said my dear sweet Monty was off his leash, she'd stalk me until she saw him off his leash. Then she'd go run and file a report." Her body stiffened, and she curled the loose end of the leash around her hand to make it taut. "Not that she was doing that today. I didn't see her until Monty made it to the fountain for a drink."

"Was Monty off his leash?" I asked.

Layla looked left and then right before she looked back at me. She sucked both sides of her cheeks in like she was contemplating telling me the truth.

"No. In fact"—she rolled her eyes upward—"he'd jumped in the fountain, and I found him licking her face. Her dead face." She tugged the leash closer to her body before she leaned in and whispered, "Rosey Hume would die if she knew that Monty had licked her dead body, and she'd die if she knew that's the last thing people would remember if it got out. I'm begging you not to write that."

Rhett's lips pulled in tight.

"It'll be our little secret." I winked but still made the note.

"Good. Now I know this may seem unkind, but I hope the murder won't affect any of our other events. We have such a lot planned." She nodded.

"We are still doing the fountain," Rhett confirmed.

"I'm guessing it's Melissa Mann coming to do it, because she called me yesterday to get her on a plane back to Holiday Junction, since I'm her travel agent and all." Layla could prove to be really helpful when it came to who was on the plane with me and Jay Mann.

"About that." I flipped the notepad to a different page. "Can you tell me if you know offhand who from Holiday Junction was on the airplane with me? I'm also looking into Jay's murder."

"There's been so many people trying to get here for the Shamrock Festival, I can't remember who was on what flights, but if you stop by my office, I can take a look for you. Rhett knows where it is. He can show you. Right, Rhett?"

"Yes, ma'am." The polite side of him came out, taking me a bit off guard.

"Oh, and you need to look at Zack. If anyone could connect these two murders, he'd be it. He made all kinds of threats to people during Hibernian meetings. I know this is the busiest time of the year for them, but he's got a very short fuse, and when it gets lit, Layla was the only one who could put it out. And let's just say when the fuse was lit because of her, there was no hope for her until he calmed down." The more Layla talked, the more I was interested in learning about Zack Hume.

"Thank you. We might be stopping by your office," I told her before Rhett and I walked away. "Now. Where do I get a copy of that paper?" I asked Rhett.

CHAPTER TWELVE

"I t's a small dying paper. Who cares?" Rhett tried to talk me out of going to get a copy of the paper.

"I care." I stalked out of the park and onto the sidewalk, heading back to the main street. "It might be a dying paper, but it still has a presence. It can take one article being picked up by the Associated Press to bring life back into a dying newspaper, and I don't want to be that one article."

I'd already dodged one bullet from the live broadcast from the airport where all of my makeup had run down my face and my hair was a mess, since the circumstances of finding a dead body and putting it aside to go live did save me some face.

Though I'd become an immediate meme afterwards, I was now being seen as a journalist who put aside her emotions to bring the story to the national news, and my live had been seen over two million times. That was a number I was sure was going to give Richard Stone the confidence he needed to hire me without me actually going to the rescheduled interview.

"Which way to the newspaper office?" I asked.

"Office?" he asked back.

"Yeah. Office." I pulled my phone out to see if Richard Stone had texted me back since I'd sent him ten text messages to confirm a reschedule.

Nothing.

"It's a decent-sized walk that way." Rhett pointed down the street.

"Past the Jubilee Inn?" I was trying to get a feel for how long it would take since I knew it took ten minutes to walk to the park from the inn.

Time was of the essence when it came to breaking news. A good reporter knew how to use her time efficiently, and while I had to be here, I could work on perfecting my skills so I would be in high performance mode when I got to my first day on the new job.

"Yes." He walked in that direction.

"Are you going with me?" I asked.

"I don't have anything else to do but go to the fun festival things. I'll tag along." He patted his stomach. "Have you eaten?"

"Kristine brought me some breakfast, but I only had time to eat the toast." I didn't want to tell him that I felt a little hungover.

"What else can you do to celebrate St. Patrick's Day around here?" I shouldn't've asked.

"Well, yesterday was the beginning of the fun. Violet Rhinehammer, you might be mad about your little layover here, but it's probably the best time to visit. Well, not unless you're here for Fourth of July. That's a much better celebration, if you ask me." He yammered on about the festival while I wanted to let him know that I'd be far away from here by July fourth.

"Over there behind Sharmel's Hardware in the parking lot are the amusement rides. They are open this week from five to ten p.m., but if you purchase an armband for seventeen dollars, you get unlimited rides all week."

"Oh goody," I said with a little snark.

"Even if you don't like amusement park rides, the money goes to the Mother's Day festival. This year they are calling it Tea Time." He put his finger up to his mouth. "That's a well-kept secret, so don't tell anyone, or the Daisy Ladies will have a fit."

"We can't upset the Daisy Ladies, now can we?" I didn't know who the Daisy Ladies were, but I didn't plan on giving their little Mother's Day festival another thought.

Ever.

"Then we have the beer garden along with many arts and crafts vendors, not to mention the delicious food." He was trying too hard to convince me how great the Shamrock Festival was and how lucky I was to be here.

"I've had enough of beer for a year. Possibly two." My stomach did somersaults at the mere mention of beer.

"I know beer's not your thing. What about music?" He walked sideways next to me as we passed festival goers.

"I do love music." I did, and taking in some live music did have some appeal to me.

"Then you don't want to miss the Emerald Stage today. The Mad Fiddlers are amazing. I'm hungry. Do you want a donut?" He indicated taking a pit stop at a food vendor stand.

"No. I'll wait here." I stayed on the sidewalk and let him fight the crowd to get a donut. Must be some good donuts, but I was really watching what went into my mouth. The beers were calories I sure didn't need, and it would take a day or so to get the inflammation I was feeling in my fingers to go down so I wouldn't look like a sausage on camera when Richard gave me my segment.

The thought of getting my own segment because of my amazing investigation work here in Holiday Junction excited me to no end.

"Excuse me." I apologized and took a couple of steps back when I realized I was in the way of people walking.

"Emily's Treasures." I read the sign after I'd turned around to face a display window.

Though it was a little gaudy, it was still cute with the shamrock lights all around the window and four-leaf clovers hanging down from the ceiling.

There was a similar dress to the one Rosey Hume was found dead in on display, as well as a man's outfit. The green coat had four-leaf clovers and a pocket square that looked exactly like the ones on Jay Mann's and Rosey Hume's dead bodies.

I hurried through the door, where a couple of musical chimes that sounded an awful lot like an Irish jig rang out.

"We can customize it for every holiday here in Holiday Junction." The woman must've seen my expression. "Welcome to Emily's Treasures. I'm Emily. What can I help you find? You must be a size six."

"Hi, Emily. Actually I'm a size four." Maybe a size four on a good day, but she wasn't ever going to see me again.

"Really? Hhhmm." Her head tilted. The wiggly four-leaf clovers on the wires of the headband in her hair went along with the green plaid shirt, khaki pants, and duck boots. "I'm usually spot-on. Must be the pint of beer I had last night."

By the way she said beer, I knew she recognized me.

"I was hoping you could give me some information on a pocket square." I opened my purse as I walked to the middle of the small boutique so I could pull out the square to show her what I was talking about.

There was a look of shock on her face.

"I wasn't expecting you to come in here for that." A brow rose with interest. "I thought you were going to come in here and ask me some questions for your investigative reporting."

She picked up something off the counter and tossed it in the small trash can next to the counter.

"Was that today's paper?" I had a very keen interest in seeing it.

"There's nothing in it. It's practically shut down for business. What is it you'd like to know?" She tried her best to get my attention away from going straight to the trash can.

"I'd still like to take a look." I shrugged, reaching down to pick it up before she gave it a good shove with her shoe.

"I don't want you to look at it." Her gaze shifted over my head. I swirled around to look, and Rhett was standing at the door, doing the whole finger-across-the-neck thing.

"He doesn't want me to look at it." I hurried over to the trash can now on its side with all the contents out around it. "I just want to look at the paper."

I carefully shoved the pocket square back in my purse and flicked the creased-in-half newspaper open.

That's when I came face-to-face with the photo of myself that was not the greatest, nor was the headline. It was from the beer contest. I had my mouth wide open, about to chug the beer. My eyes looked as if I were possessed, and my hair stuck out like my finger was jammed in a light socket. Not my finest moment.

Snooping Tourist: Holiday Junction beware!

"For the love of God, who wrote this?" I demanded an answer by just reading the headline alone.

"Now calm down, Violet. This is just the *Junction Journal*, and I told you it's on its last legs." Rhett's words brushed right on past me.

"Meddling? Dottie Swaggert called me a meddler?" I aimed my stare at Rhett. "She's one to talk!" I realized I was screaming when a customer came out of the dressing room and bolted out the door.

"I'm going to have to ask you to leave. You're scaring my clients." The woman shot darts out of her eyes at me. Not literally, but you get the picture.

"I'm sorry. But whoever wrote this piece went all the way back to my hometown to get statements from people who weren't always a fan of me." I said it in such a way that Rhett would know the people in the piece weren't always on the up-and-up. "In fact, this Dottie and her group of friends, they call themselves the Laundry Club Ladies. Really? Who on earth hangs out in a laundromat because they want to?"

"It was good to see you, Emily." Rhett had grabbed me by the arm and tried to lead me out, but I stuck in my heels, jerked my arm away, and took a deep breath.

"I'm sorry I scared off a customer." I was keenly aware of the other eyes upon me that belonged to a few people sort of hiding behind a clothing rack. "This is not a portrayal of who I am. I'm a little on edge, finding a dead body and all."

Rhett and Emily traded looks.

"I'm fine," I assured both of them. "I will read the rest of this later." I wagged the piece of garbage in the air and put it in my purse in exchange for the pocket square. "If I was so awful as that terrible article claims, then why would Chief Strickland have me looking into his case?"

"To get you out of his hair?" Emily muttered and busied herself with the piece of clothing the customer I'd scared off had left behind. "This was a two-hundred-dollar piece. That would've paid for Katie's piano lessons."

I looked at Rhett.

"Her daughter." He explained who Katie was.

"Again, I apologize." I walked back over to the counter and looked at the clothing. The sleeveless V-neck dress looked like a leprechaun had thrown up on it. It was this awful green plaid with four-leaf clovers sewn down the sides.

I set the pocket square on the counter and held my hand out.

"I'd love to try it on."

"It's a size six, and you told me you were a four." Emily was holding her ground.

"I'll take my chances." I gestured for her to give it to me. "Now while I try this on, why don't you tell me about Jay Mann coming in here and buying one of the pocket squares from you."

I headed back to the dressing room and kept the door cracked so I could hear what she had to say and prayed Rhett was listening.

"He didn't buy them from me." Emily didn't appear to want to give up any information.

"Really? What about Rosey Hume?" I asked with my mouth up to the crack in the door and started to undress.

"She didn't either." Emily wasn't any help.

I looked in the mirror and wanted to gag. I'd never be caught in something like this, much less something like this that was going to cost me two hundred dollars. But I knew if I didn't, Emily would stay tight-lipped.

There was some whispering between Rhett and her that I caught on my way out of the dressing room.

"I'm sorry, I didn't hear what you two were discussing." I made it clear I wasn't dumb and knew they were talking about me. "Now—" I opened my purse and took out two hundred dollars, knowing money was going to be tight until I got to California and Richard put me on payroll.

Maybe he could give me a starting bonus since I was proving myself to be really valuable.

I set the money on the counter. Emily eyeballed it and then me.

"I knew you were a size six." She gave me a sly smile. "Anyways, I do keep a record of who buys what. These are made locally, and neither of them bought one. But I do recall someone placing an online order from Jay's company. They bought two."

Now we were getting somewhere.

"His company?" I looked over my left shoulder at Rhett.

"I'll tell you about it on the way to the *Junction Journal*," he said, making eye contact again with Emily.

"You said these are made locally." I put the fabric square back in my purse. "Who makes them?"

"Leni McKenna."

"I know that name." I looked at Rhett again.

"The dancer from yesterday. The one who made the shamrock dresses."

"The one I saw push Rosey Hume after they had some words?" I questioned, knowing things really had gotten interesting.

CHAPTER THIRTEEN

"I'm guessing you know this Leni McKenna," I assumed after Rhett and I left Emily's Treasures.

The stares I got as we walked down the street in the direction of where Rhett said the office for the *Junction Journal* was located made me a little self-conscious.

"Yep. I do." He stopped at another vendor along the way down to the offices of the *Junction Journal*. "We will take two." He pulled some cash out of the front pocket of his jeans.

"I'm not hungry," I told him and tried to figure out the timing of all this and how it was going.

While he waited for whatever he was getting to eat, I got my phone out of my purse and checked to see if Richard Stone had called or texted.

He hadn't.

I dialed him.

"Hi, Richard. It's Violet. There's been two murders involving two people from Holiday Junction. I really think this story is getting much bigger than just Jay Mann murdered on an airplane." I pulled the phone from my mouth when I noticed Cherise, the flight attendant, standing near one of the band stages. "I have some interesting details that look like they're tied to the case. In fact, the main officer here, I guess he'd be the chief, has asked me to look into some details. He had checked out my past, and I have glowing reviews from Sheriff Hemmer in Normal."

I was really talking myself up. I had no clue what Al Hemmer had even told Matthew, but how I was asked to assist in solving the murders here had to be a good sign.

"I'm sure you're so busy getting my salary and bonus structure aligned"—I threw in the bonus thing because I needed it after all the work I was doing, and this dress I was wearing for the good of the investigation—"that you're not able to take my call when I do call. I have my phone on me now, and it's fully charged. Let me know what direction you want me to take on this murder investigation, since it looks like I'm stuck here another day."

I had made it across the street and over to where Cherise was standing out of her uniform. She looked way better than the day I'd seen her. She had a huge smile on her face, and her hair that had been up in a bun was now flowing down her back. The uniform did nothing for her long legs that went for miles in her red capri pants and thin arms that poked out of the sleeves of her snug white sweater.

"Oh my. Look at you, Violet." Cherise turned with a beer in her hand. "You have drunk the Shamrock Festival juice."

She looked me up and down with her assessing eyes.

"You wouldn't even believe it if I told you." I sucked in a deep breath. "Do you have any idea when they are going to let us leave?"

"No clue about your flight, but I'm on a flight tomorrow heading east." She smiled and pointed to the man next to her. "This is Patrick. I think you met him when he picked me up at the airport."

The eyes. I recognized the eyes. They'd locked lips before he zoomed off.

"No, I didn't. Hi, Patrick. I'm Violet." I took a side step to let Rhett in when he walked up.

"Yeah. Yeah. I remember you." He lifted his chin and put his arm around Cherise. The look he gave Rhett didn't go unnoticed.

"Hey, Patrick. Cherise," Rhett greeted them. "Here you go." He held out a brown paper napkin with a slice of baguette. "Irish soda bread. You're going to love it."

"On your hips," Cherise noted with raised brows.

"Are you ready? We need to get to the paper." Rhett nudged me and moved back in with the crowd.

"Nice to meet you." I gave them a wave before I turned to scan over top the crowd's heads to see where Rhett had gone.

"Welcome to Emerald Stage the Mad Fiddlers!" the announcer screamed over the microphone before electric fiddles took over.

"Hey!" I tried to yell at Rhett, but the Mad Fiddlers had started to sing, and, well, the crowd was going crazy.

Rhett had gotten back on the sidewalk, which was a lot less crowded and rowdy. I wasn't sure if selling beer all day was a great idea, but then again, I had no idea what Holiday Junction was like. All I knew was there were two murders that appeared to be tied and the Village newspaper was single-handedly ruining my career.

"Hey." I put my hand on Rhett's arm after I'd finally caught up to him. "Isn't this the band you wanted me to hear?"

"It's too crowded. Besides"—he put the end of the Irish soda bread in his mouth and bit off a piece—"we need to get to the *Junction Journal* before they close."

"Do you forget who you're dealing with?" I asked. "I'm an investigative reporter."

"I thought you were a journalist, Violet. Which is it? Investigative reporter or journalist?" He stopped with a look on his face that was so sore and mean.

"I see." It occurred to me that his personality had changed as soon as he found me with Patrick and Cherise. "What was the deal with you, Patrick, and Cherise?"

"There is no deal. Those two drive me nuts." Rhett held something close to his chest.

"How do you know them?" I asked.

"We live here. We grew up together." He took one more bite before he started to walk again. "Aren't you going to eat your bread?"

The Jubilee Inn was across the street, so I kinda knew where I was but still didn't know where the office for the *Junction Journal* was.

"I'm not much on carbs." I had to dig deeper. I knew he was holding something back.

"Trust me. You're going to love it." He took another bite along with making bigger strides in his gait.

It took two of my steps to keep up with his one, and before I could look up, we were rounding the corner away from the shops and going to where the big houses were located.

"You three didn't seem to get along very well. And it has to be something if you suddenly changed your mind about this awesome band you insisted I check out."

He abruptly stopped in front of a gate with a large brick wall on each side.

"There was too big of a crowd. We can listen to Patrick any ole day. He's my brother." He pointed to the red-brick home off in the distance behind the gate. "That's where the *Junction Journal* offices are."

"And they are going under?" I questioned.

"You could say that." He tapped a code into the silver box, and the gates opened.

"Here's a thought." I followed him inside. "They should sell this land to keep the *Junction Journal* afloat."

"I don't think it's about money. I think it's about age." He didn't make any sense. The *New York Times* started way back in the mid eighteen-hundreds.

"Too bad the thing wasn't dead before I got here," I said.

He stopped abruptly again and looked at me.

"What? It wasn't a flattering photo, nor was the article nice." I shrugged then muttered, "They deserve to not be printed."

Rhett continued to walk up the long brick sidewalk. The tall trees stood along each side with their fresh new spring leaves. I was a sucker for nature. I grew up in the Daniel Boone National Forest, where the seasons made the most beautiful landscape. Not a single photographer could come close to getting a picture to capture its true beauty.

This place would also give photographers a run for their money with the manicured lawn and the perfectly trimmed shrubs. I tried not to fall over my own feet when I twisted around to look back at that brick wall on this side of the street, which was lined with gorgeous hedges.

"Do you get all four seasons here in Holiday Junction?" I knew I'd made him upset about nosing into his relationship with Patrick and Cherise as well as the paper, or maybe he was just sensitive to the fact it was his home.

I knew better, and, well, as they say at home, it's easier to get something with honey. So I decided right then and there to put my nice foot forward. It shouldn't be too hard since I wasn't staying here much longer.

It was for the good of the story. Right?

"I swear I've died, because I know that's not you walking up on my front porch, Rhett Strickland." The older woman was sitting in one of the egg chairs hanging down from the large front porch of the offices of the *Junction Journal*.

"You've not died. I've brought a friend." He motioned for the old woman not to get up and hurried over to give her a kiss.

Unusual greeting for even a southerner like me.

"Nah. I'm getting up to greet any friend of yours." She wasn't feeble at all. She popped right up out of the egg chair and adjusted the brown shawl draped over her shoulders. Her hair was all silver and cut into a bob, neatly styled.

The outfit she had on was more of a lounging outfit, a cream matching top and bottom. She had on a pair of jeweled sandals that I felt it was too cold for, but then again, what did I know? I'd just spent a fortune on the silly dress I was wearing.

She gave me an odd look then took the glasses dangling from the chain around her neck. Putting them on, a smile grew on her face.

"You look nothing like the photo printed in today's *Junction Journal*." She grinned and slid her eyes to Rhett.

"That's why we are here. I'm demanding a retraction from the editor in chief." I crossed my arms and did a little stomp with my foot. "I mean you no disrespect, ma'am, but I certainly will not let a newspaper, if you call it that, such as the *Junction Journal* try to ruin my career. You have no idea where I'm going and how much this little murdery situation you have in your town." I stopped with my fists to my side. "Village," I corrected myself, "has cost me."

"You've got some spunk. We need spunk around here." She sighed and paid what I'd just said no attention whatsoever.

"I'm sorry?" I questioned.

"Honey, don't be sorry for that spunky go-getter attitude. I had one of those myself back when I was your age." She made no sense.

Then it dawned on me. She had dementia.

"Yes. Well, if you'll excuse us, we have some business with the paper." I tugged on Rhett's arm on my way to the door so I could march right on in and get them to retract that story.

When I entered the office building, I figured I'd be hearing someone, anyone, on a phone, computer keys clacking, maybe a printer or two. A newsroom at the least.

"Hi there!" This woman greeted me from a room to the right. She was lounging on a couch. "You must be from the Hibernians. Let me get you a donation. I sure hated to hear about Jay and Rosey." She got up and put her feet in a pair of slippers. She wore a bright-green dress, no doubt matching the festive occasion, and had silver hair.

It made me wish that I would look as pretty as she did when I was her age.

"I'm here to see the editor in chief about the *Junction Journal* and a retraction for the awful story written about me in this morning's paper." I looked around at the decorated crown molding, chandeliers, and the fancy furniture.

The credenza was filled with picture frames, and one face in particular I recognized.

Rhett Strickland.

CHAPTER FOURTEEN

"You brought me to your family's home?" I questioned Rhett through my gritted teeth with a smile hiding those. "I thought we were going to go to the offices of *Junction Journal?*"

"We did." He shrugged and looked at the two women standing in front of us in the fancy family room that looked more like a museum than a home.

I might be from a small Kentucky town, but I knew what high-end décor, custom window treatments, and expensive area rugs looked like from the magazines I'd thumb through when I stood in line at the grocery store.

"Did I blink?" I was curious as to how I missed the offices of the newspaper.

"You just met her." He pointed to the older woman. "That's my aunt Marge and my aunt Louise. They both run the *Junction Journal* right here from their home."

"With the internet these days, it's so easy to grab what we need and zip it on over to the printing press, where we've got Clara and Garnett Ness not only printing off *Junction Journal*, but their boy delivers it for us." Aunt Marge was the one I'd met outside. "That's how I know who you are, Violet Rhinehammer."

"Violet Rhinehammer?" Aunt Louise took an interest and walked over to join us. "I see." She drew a curious look from Rhett to me. She wagged a finger between us. "You two know each other enough to be gallivanting around town?"

"We aren't gallivanting." I didn't like the way she said it because it insinuated something more was taking place.

"Oh, you're definitely gallivanting, because I heard from Kristine from the Jubilee Inn, and she did tell me about you two then. Of course, I had to see who was at the Shamrock Festival Stein Competition so I could get those in the paper." Aunt Louise drummed her fingers together.

"Why on earth would you print something as awful as saying I was drunk and then go as far as saying that I wasn't a good reporter?" I was on the verge of crying.

"I didn't say that." Louise drew back and looked at Marge. "Did we say that?"

"No way. I edited the piece several times after you wrote it, and we sure did not print that." Marge shook her head. "I think we might've said something about the drinking, and we might've..." She hesitated and waved her hand. "Don't you pay no attention to the *Junction Journal*. Just like you mentioned underneath your breath, we seem to be on our last legs."

For an older woman, she sure did have good hearing.

"Why is that?" I looked around and pointed to a fancy painting on the wall. "I am sure you could auction that off and get a pretty enough penny to sustain the paper."

"Why do you care?" Marge asked.

"Aunts," Rhett interrupted.

"No, Rhett." Marge put a stiff finger up to him, and he retreated. "Let her answer." She followed up with a stern look.

"You said it. The internet has everything, but the newspaper is dying, and there's something about a small newspaper where you can see the obituaries, like Jay and now Rosey." I could see the emotions in both of their faces shift when I mentioned Rosey.

It appeared they'd not yet been privy to the information.

"Along with photos of weddings, birth announcements, and such keepsakes people love to cut out, put in albums." I knew these were very old-fashioned and not keeping up with the times. I didn't keep any of those, and I was still in my twenties, but my family did.

Heck, there were groups of my friends who spent a mint on scrapbooking materials and even hosted these crazy parties.

"Are you telling me that you have decided to stop the paper because you're tired of it?" I wanted to show them I was going to question them. "I'm sure the community has pushed back on this decision."

"They don't know. We were going to tell them at the next city council meeting." Louise held her phone in her hand and was scrolling on the screen. She didn't seem to care as much for the discussion as Marge did. "They don't fund it. So it's our decision."

"Who started the *Junction Journal*? How did you get it? Is there history there?" I asked.

"It was started by Rhett's great relatives. All of them. We've kept it in the family, but now the younger Stricklands like Rhett and Matthew, to name a couple, don't want to take over the paper. They want to do other things. Noble things like keep the Village in order. Which brings me back to what you said about Rosey. Rosey Hume?" Marge looked at Louise.

"I can't seem to find anything." Louise continued to tap at the phone.

"She was found in the park fountain with a silk pocket scarf stuffed in her mouth like the one Jay Mann had. I can see you perk up. Is your heart beating fast? The thought of you not on the big story? Big news?" I began to spout off exactly how it felt when a news story broke and you were about to write about it.

"When did this happen, and why don't we know about it?" Marge asked Louise.

"Matthew did call, but I was on the phone with Kristine," Louise said with a poker face. She looked like she was trying to remain calm.

"What time was that?" I asked.

"It was around seven a.m. Why?" Louise questioned.

"Because the murder was probably right before that, and she didn't come to my room until eight a.m. That's when she told me about Rosey, so she probably didn't know when she was on the phone with you. Which brings me back to my point." I gestured to her cell phone in her hand. "It's not on there yet, but it will be soon. You still don't have the story."

"We won't even get printed out until tomorrow since it's print." Marge lifted her hands. "Hence why we don't want to keep this thing running. If you've not noticed"—her eyes assessed me—"we are a little older than you."

"Little?" Rhett teased.

Marge smiled at him. By the way they acted toward one another, I could see there was a bond there.

"Why don't you keep the paper open and have it online?" I shrugged.

"I suggested that a year ago and even built them a site." Rhett had a know-it-all look on his face. "I love you, aunts."

"If the site is there, you can do a big print once a week, and then when stuff happens, like it did with Rosey, you can get it up and even do some marketing techniques to get the AP to pick it up." It was a no-brainer.

"You mean like you did with your video from the airport?" Marge took more of an interest in my suggestion than Louise did.

"Yes. But I was actually doing it for my job, not just some willy-nilly live from my phone." I needed to make it clear to them who they were talking to. "I'm on my way to my job, and this is just a pit stop until Matthew lets me leave."

"He told me yesterday they were starting to let people leave." By the way Louise eyeballed me, I could tell she was very leery.

"He said they were going by alphabet, and by my initials, you can see where I've always fallen—at the bottom." That did garner a couple of snorts from them, letting me know I had penetrated some part of their human side. Not the stiff newspaper side that takes years to develop.

"Uncle Matthew has Violet on the case as well. Just as a liaison type,"

Rhett told them. "Just while she's here. You know, since she's got the skills to find things out."

"Is that right?" Marge walked next to me and slipped her hand in the crook of my elbow. "Then I have a proposition for you."

"Aunt Marge, you can't possibly." Rhett tried to intervene again without success. "Fine. I'll stay out of it."

"What if you do a little write-up about yourself, and that's how we will fix our little article about you." Marge was sweet-talking me. The whole honey thing that I was supposed to be doing to them, they were doing to me.

But I was all ears. I did love a good sweet-talking.

"Then you write up a little article about what you saw on the airplane with Jay Mann. Interview a couple of passengers before Matthew lets them leave."

"I can interview Cherise. She was with me the entire time." The mere mention of the woman made her jaw drop. "Or not."

"You can interview whomever you want. You were on the plane, and they were too." Louise had bought into whatever Marge was selling me.

I listened with caution.

"Then you make a little write-up about your thoughts as an outsider during the Shamrock Festival."

"I don't think you want me to do that because I think it's all wrong how the police officers stayed off duty during the parade while a murder had been committed. Technically it wasn't committed here, but the plane landed here." I was making sense of it in my head.

"Are you sure it wasn't committed here?" Marge asked. "Louise, get the file."

"But..." Louise hesitated.

"We can trust her." Marge had more secrets and moves up her sleeve than I'd figured. "After you look over the file, then we want you to post to the online website Rhett built for us. He can give you the login." She shot him a look.

"Put your articles on there. We will call it a guest reporting appearance until you get the green light from Matthew to leave." Louise was all too happy to add more instructions for me.

These Strickland propositions were starting to make me think something fishy was going on. I didn't know what, but there was something.

It tickled my fancy, and, well, what was one more thing to take on while I was held captive in this kookie town?

There were two things I had to agree with—use their home as my office and come for the family supper tonight.

CHAPTER FIFTEEN

There was a stack of papers in the file Marge and Louise Strickland had given me. It was something I wasn't going to be able to get through while I was there. It was going to take some time, and, well, I still had my own little investigation going, which left me zero time if I was going to go see Leni McKenna, the tailor who made the dress Rosey had on and the pocket squares found on the two victims.

I had agreed to Marge and Louise's terms only because they seemed to think the murders were related, like me, plus they had a pulse on this town. They were in the know and part of one of the largest families in Holiday Junction.

"Now what?" Rhett asked me.

"Don't you have a job to do?" I asked him in hopes he'd let me work alone.

"I'm offended, Violet Rhinehammer. I've practically given you a job to do while you are here. Do you really think Uncle Matthew would let any old person, much less an outsider, snoop around without some coaxing? Do you really think he's good at looking people up on the internet and getting phone numbers to check people out?" He told me without really telling me that it was him that got Matthew in touch with Al Hemmer. "Besides, the airport is still closed down until Matthew opens it."

"What about the other passengers cleared to leave?" I asked.

"They are being bused to Banchester. That's really where most of the flights leave in and out from."

"Yeah, that's where I was making a connection." I recalled how I'd gotten on the airport website to see if I had to hustle from one terminal to the other. It was only a tad bit bigger than Holiday Junction. "You only work at the airport security?"

"Is that a problem?" he questioned. "Does that make me less-than in your eyes?"

"Don't take it so personal." I followed him down the front steps of his aunts' home and back down the way we came, through the gates that put us back on the street. "I'm used to working alone, that's all. Not having a shadow."

"That's what Matthew wants. But if it makes you feel better, after we go see Leni, I do have to be somewhere." He didn't offer where, and I didn't ask, thinking the time away from him could be when I'd look over the file from his aunts, which I'd stuffed in my purse.

"Where is Leni's shop?" I wondered before we turned down a little side street with smaller houses with nice-size yards.

Unlike the outside of the aunts' house, these houses had all the décor for the festival. They had stringy lights in the shape of shamrocks, and some had green streamers hanging down off their house. Their front shrubs were decorated like you'd do a Christmas tree, and some even had their windows painted green.

"The Lucky Leprechaun showed up here." He grinned and pointed to a life-sized Leprechaun with a big joker-type smile on its face at the top of the street. "Every year the Lucky Leprechaun shows up in a neighborhood. That's the Lucky Leprechaun. We don't know who does it, but it happens at Easter, Thanksgiving, Christmas, any holiday with a mascot. If the mascot of that holiday shows up in your neighborhood, the residents have to host some sort of community party in celebration."

"And you want me to write an article on this?" I asked. "Or is Leni's shop in her house too?"

"No. I live down here, and we are going to get my car." He shook his head. "Violet Rhinehammer, you are so uptight. Did you know that?"

I didn't say a word, even though I wanted to. I decided to keep my mouth shut. I waited outside of his house and wondered how much money a security guard at the Holiday Junction airport made, because it looked really nice from the outside. He had minimal decorations on the front, and by minimal, I mean he had a green rug in front of his door and two green pillows on the porch swing. Other than that, he didn't have any more Shamrock Festival decorations.

He didn't invite me in, and I didn't just walk in like we did back home. It didn't stop me from glancing into the windows, and I noticed he had leather furniture and nice pieces of other things. He didn't have much on the walls as in decorations, and he didn't seem to have any knickknack-type things sitting around there.

Pretty minimalist.

When the car horn honked, I jumped around.

"I don't know why I'd be surprised you were a peeping Tom," he called from the convertible, which made me think of Fern. "You could've come in."

"I'm not a peeping Tom," I said when I got into the car and slammed the door. "It's rude not to be invited, so you should've invited me." After I belted up, I dug through my purse to get the pocket square.

"Fine. You can come in later." He put the car in drive, and my mind hung on his word "later."

Little did he know there wasn't going to be a later. I wasn't even planning on getting through the second article the aunts wanted me to write. Instead, I was going to get these murders solved and get out of this village for good.

"What can you tell me about Leni?" I wanted to be as prepared as possible so I didn't spend a lot of time trying to figure her out myself. I took the pocket square out.

"What's there to know? She's a seamstress, everyone goes to her, and she does some pieces that are sold locally." He nodded to the pocket square. "Like those."

"What about the community? Does she participate? Hang out with people? Have any enemies?" I threw out the typical journalist questions.

"Leni? Heck no. I mean, I guess she could rub anyone the wrong way, like all of us can." I wasn't sure, but I thought his comment was directed toward me.

The wind whipped into the car as the car sped towards the airport.

I could see the airport in the distance and wished I was in one of the sitting airplanes, ready to take off. The images only made me want to get this thing solved so I could get myself out of here, not rely on the police department or Rhett.

"I do appreciate you taking me around," I thanked him. "I'm sure you don't want to be by my side since Matthew thinks I need a babysitter."

"I'm good. I've enjoyed getting to know you." He kept his eyes on the road.

"Your aunts seem to be fun." It was actually very endearing to see how they interacted with him.

"They are a lot of fun. Don't expect that from my parents." He spoke a little louder as the wind continued to pick up.

"Your parents?" I asked, not ever intending to meet them.

"Yeah. They'll be at the aunts' for supper tonight." He refreshed my memory.

"Oh. That." My voice faded off, and I turned to take in the scenery of the mountains as well as the flat land where there was some cattle grazing. I wasn't even sure if he'd heard me.

The sun pelting down into the car actually felt good on my face. I leaned my head back against the headrest and closed my eyes.

"We're here, Violet." Rhett's voice brought me out of my nap. "Wake up, Sleeping Beauty."

I opened my eyes and literally had to stop to think about where I was and who I was with.

"You took a nice little nap." He'd already turned off the car, and we were parked in front of a small brick cottage-style house with moss growing down the front of it.

There were a couple of homemade benches with flowerpots lined up on top filled with gorgeous greenery and pops of colored petals.

The cottage was nestled in a wooded area, off the beaten path, from what I could tell, since I'd been asleep the entire time.

"What do I owe the pleasure?" A woman with super-curly brown hair who I recognized as the woman in the parade popped out the door. She had her hand over her eyes to shield the sun to look at us. "I heard the gravel spitting up, and here you are. Do I owe—" she started to say.

"I'm here for my friend Violet Rhinehammer." He interrupted her before she could go on with what she was trying to say. "She's got a couple of questions about your silk pocket squares."

We got out of the car. I walked over and showed her the shamrock one.

"Your place is adorable." It had so much charm to it. The roof was tin and green, making it blend nicely with the background.

"It's been a saving grace for me to have my space and not in my home." She pinched a grin. "Don't get me wrong. I love Vern, but once he hit retirement, and, well, since the holidays are far between, he gets a little bored. He wants to travel here and there and everywhere." She looked down at the pocket square. "I loved making those. Who are you giving it to?"

"Giving it to?" I asked.

"Mmhmmm." She gave a few quick nods. "I'm guessing you bought it from Emily's Treasures. That's the only place I wholesale for during any holiday event. I don't make much off her, but the customers do like my quality of work, and they take my business card. They always call for more but different patterns." She waved us to follow her inside. "That's where I make up the money I lose when I mark items down for Emily."

"I was hoping you'd be able to tell us if you knew who purchased them from Jay Mann's office. She said they were anonymously ordered and sent to Jay Mann's office. That's why I wondered if anyone from his office bought them. Or just the small community say something to you?"

"My, that's a lot to take in. I have no idea who bought them." She shook her head.

The inside of the one-room cottage was literally filled with hooks on the wall with spools and spools of yarn and threads. She had one sewing machine in the middle, where there was a piece of cloth in position under the threading needle. It had to be the fabric she'd been working on when we got there.

Leni went back to the sewing machine, where she began to sew on whatever was stuck up under the needle. She glided the fabric through with ease as the machine put in stitch after stitch.

"Are you a member of the Hibernian Society?" I knew she was because she was in the parade.

"Me and most people in the Holiday Junction." She made it sound like a very dumb question. "Until someone gets mad and quits."

"Did you go to the last meeting?" I asked. "I understand the two victims had gotten into an argument. And I was wondering what that was about."

"Two victims." She stopped the machine and put her hands in her lap, looking up at me. "They are our friends. If you're going to be here, you need to know that no matter what kind of scuffles or arguments we get into, at the end of the day, we are friends. We've been living here a very long time. They have names. Jay and Rosey."

"I'm sorry. I didn't mean to upset you." I could tell she was visibly shaken by my comments. "If you can believe it, I'm from a town smaller than Holiday Junction."

This was when I knew I had to show my personal side instead of the journalist side. Like Mae had said, be part of the community while I was here, not as if I just wanted to take something from them.

"I have no idea what they were discussing. I'm not sure what you heard, but it wasn't an argument. They were talking in the corner, and from what it looked like, it did seem to be something of importance, but I wasn't sure what. I didn't ask. It was over before the meeting got started and nothing mentioned after that."

There was a bark outside of the shop. I glanced out and noticed it was Layla Camsen again and her dog.

"Layla never shuts that dog up." Leni went back to the sewing machine. "I drown the thing out by working. It's hard since she lives on the property next door."

"Next door?" I looked at Rhett. "I thought she took the dog..." I started to tell Layla's story from this morning because I was confused about the walking path she took with her dog.

"The park is right through the woods in the back of Layla's house. Holiday Junction might look really big, but it's not. Every wooded area connects to somewhere in the Village, and the seaside is that way."

"My goodness. I'm going to need a map," I joked. I turned back to Leni. "Did you happen to hear anything unusual this morning?"

Layla stopped sewing for a brief moment. She gave a slow nod.

"I did hear this strange squeaking noise coming from the woods, but I never looked out. I was too busy trying to get ready for Mother's Day. I get a lot of requests for aprons." She pointed to a table next to the sewing machine with some finished aprons she'd made.

"You're the second person to mention the squeak."

"I was thinking it was Layla's gardener. He's always crossing the property line and planting new rose bushes for Layla since she's the president of the Ladies of Mother Earth, our local gardening club. She believes she has to have the best roses and keep her appearance up for her presidency." Leni gave me someone else to look at. "Everyone told Layla she needed to purchase a new pushcart for her gardener since she insists he work for the Ladies of Mother Earth. If you ask me, she's using the funds for her own garden and not to keep Holiday Junction gorgeous."

"Do you have his name?" I asked.

"Reed Schwindt. He pretty much keeps to himself," she said.

I wrote it down in the notebook.

"Is there any way he'd have a motive to kill Jay Mann or Rosey Hume?" I asked.

She shifted her eyes to look at Rhett then back to me. She seemed to be surprised by my question.

"Reed?" She scoffed. "Are you kidding me? Have you seen him? He's creepy and has all of those knives. Plus he was fired by Jay Mann a couple of weeks ago." Her brows lifted. "I told your uncle that he needed to look at Reed."

I knew the next person I needed to see was Reed Schwindt.

"If you remember anything else, please call me. I'm staying at the Jubilee Inn until Chief Strickland clears the airplane for takeoff." I thanked her once again before Rhett and I left.

"Here you go, Rhett." She handed him a piece of paper. "You have to get the leaky—" she started to say before he interrupted her.

"I've got it." He flashed his smile, winked, and showed me to the door as he slipped the piece of paper in his pocket.

I stood outside of the door and quickly jotted down a few notes so I wouldn't forget.

"Let's go. I've got to get to the fountain." Rhett stood next to the car and opened the door.

I hurried over and got in. I had my notebook in my lap as I went over what Leni had said.

"Now what are you thinking?" Rhett asked and pulled out of the drive.

"I'm thinking I want to talk to Layla's gardener. And if Layla heard the sound, wouldn't she recognize it?" I asked. "Or was she trying to cover up it was him but also tell us it was him?"

"Loyalties do lie deep here in Holiday Junction." Rhett told me something that I was figuring out on my own and certainly something I needed to dig in deeper on.

"What did Leni mean when she asked if you were there for something?" I didn't let the little interruption in the beginning of our visit go untouched. There was something odd that Rhett didn't want me to know. It was the second time today he'd ended some conversations that pertained to him.

"I have no idea." He shrugged, keeping his eye on the road.

"What was on the piece of paper?" I questioned.

"Let's get you back to the Jubilee Inn so you can rest up for tonight's supper at the aunts'." He flipped on the radio and turned up the music, his way of telling me he didn't want to talk.

CHAPTER SIXTEEN

I didn't head into the Jubilee Inn. I knew it was getting close to the Greening of the Fountain ceremony, and I didn't want to miss it. Not only for the fact that I'd never seen anything like this and while I was here I might'swell go, but the bigger factor was I knew from years of investigative reporting—to be honest and clear, I'd never really done a lot of it, but from what I had done—it was possible the killer could return to the scene of the crime.

It was sort of a sick way for them to see how things played out.

And by the looks of the crowd, everyone was as curious as me. I walked around with my phone on video so I could take screenshots of what I needed for my big article for the aunts for the *Junction Journal*.

I made my way to the front of the fountain and slowly turned around in a circle to take in the masses of people that'd come out to see the annual festivity. Leni along with Layla was in a huddle with a couple of people on one side of the fountain. On the opposite side was Rhett, Chief Strickland, Fern, and the two aunts.

I shifted my focus to the far side of the fountain, where I recognized Kristine, Cherise, and Patrick. I found it very interesting Cherise and Patrick weren't next to Rhett.

There appeared to be a heavier police presence than there was earlier, and all of the police seemed to be alert. When I heard the Irish band playing, I looked up and saw Fern leading the small parade down the large sidewalk. They appeared to be going to the fountain.

She had on another fancy green dress with a huge sash stating her title. A few times she bent down to greet little girls in awe of her as well as blow a few kisses in the air to men whistling at her.

Our eyes locked when she passed, and she smirked before she continued to lead the band, the group of men who all wore Hibernian sashes, and a couple of women and a little girl, who I assumed were Jay Mann's family.

Melissa Mann's eyes were dark underneath, and the red line on the bottom lid showed she'd been crying, though she was trying to put on a brave face. Their daughter didn't seem to be able to have that in her as the tears continued to flow in silence. The granddaughter kept hold of her mother's hand. From what I understood, she was ill, and from her thin, skeletal body, I could tell what I'd heard was true.

My emotions were already on high alert, forcing me to look down when they passed by me. The rush of sadness formed like a hard ball in my throat. I gulped several times to dampen the feelings before the tears started to burn in my eyes.

It was a heartbreaking scene on such a wonderful day for the community.

Following the Manns, I noticed another man with a bouquet of daisies dyed green. He, too, looked as if he'd been crying, and I wondered if it was Rosey's husband.

He kept his eyes on the fountain and didn't look around, so I wasn't forced to look away when he passed. There was one last man in a kilt holding a baton, signaling the end of the small parade to the ceremony.

I took out my notebook and jotted down the emotions, not only what I was feeling but my observation of the family. It was going to be rare material for my article and something I wanted to put into my broadcast I was sending Richard Stone.

While the people partaking in the ceremony got settled and the microphone got set up, the crowd gathered around the fountain. I took a few snapshots that might or might not go into the article, but they would give me the scene to help me describe it.

"Welcome to the Greening of the Fountain!" The crowd roared to life as the man spoke into the microphone. "We would like to welcome Mayor Paisley"—he gestured to the side, where I hadn't noticed Kristine and Paisley had taken a spot—"as well as our city council members."

While he rattled off the city council members' names, I weaved myself in and out of the crowd so I could get as close as possible to the front to get a few snapshots. Mayor Paisley was dressed in a little dress made with a four-leaf clover pattern. It was the cutest thing, and a photo of her was a must.

"As you know, we have lost two of our Hibernian Society members, and their families are here today in recognition and support." The man gestured to the group behind him. "Zack Hume, the husband of Rosey Hume, our society secretary, will now lay flowers in the fountain in her memory."

A silence fell over the crowd. There were a few sniffles echoing around me. Everyone's eyes focused on the ground, and I took a few photos of Zack Hume walking up to the fountain and placing the flowers in the fountain.

He took a step back into the parade group.

There were a few more moments of silence before the man stepped back up to the microphone.

"As you know, Jay Mann was the master of ceremonies today. I'm honored to be able to step into Jay's shoes. I know they are going to be hard to fill, and I will try my best." Immediately Jay Mann's family stepped up to join the man, along with another man dressed in a kilt with a society sash on. He held out a book of sorts, as though they were going to do a swearing-in ceremony.

"Please repeat after me," the man with the book said. "I, state your name."

"I, Vern McKenna." His words popped my eyes open.

Vern McKenna as in Leni's husband? I wondered, scanning the crowd to see if she was there.

Deep in the crowd I saw her standing with a huge smile on her face.

Out of the corner of my eye, there was a movement. I looked back and noticed Zack Hume had left the ceremony, walking down the side-walk that led to the seaside.

The swearing-in ceremony was giving Vern the presidential seat of the society.

"As your newly elected president, I'd like to have a moment of silence for Jay Mann." Vern had taken the ceremony over and led the group in a little prayer before he introduced Melissa, Sandra, and Dana Mann.

None of them spoke but only gave a slight wave with a solemn expression on their faces. My heart dropped looking at them, and I captured the moment on video.

"Since it's my privilege to do the honors of greening the fountain, this year I'd like to hand the duties over to Jay's legacy, his granddaughter, Dana Mann." By the way the Mann family was taken by surprise, Vern had not informed them of his plan.

The crowd erupted, but the little girl didn't understand. Sandra bent down and whispered into her daughter's ear as she pointed to the small green water pitcher. The little girl's eyes grew, her head bobbled, and her body began to bounce in excitement.

The society members gathered around the fountain as Sandra and Melissa stood on each side of little Dana, both holding her hands as they led her up to the edge of the fountain. The bagpipes rang out while the little girl dropped her family's grip and took the water can from Vern.

He bent over and said a few words to the little girl. Dana nodded in agreement before Vern straightened up and gave her the go-ahead.

Melissa and Sandra, though they still looked grief stricken, had some pride glowing on their faces as they watched Jay's granddaughter fulfill something so special to Holiday Junction.

My phone captured the moment, and in no time, all the water was green.

"Excuse me. Excuse me." I made my way past the crowd and scanned the sidewalk, going toward the seaside. I was looking for Zack Hume, but he was gone.

I found myself continuing toward the seaside and looked back at the crowd at the fountain, where the bagpipes had started to play. It looked as though Melissa Mann was going to speak, and though I wanted to hear what she had to say, I wanted my own interview.

I wasn't sure how to get it, so I took off to the next best interview. I was in search of Zack Hume.

CHAPTER SEVENTEEN

The sun had begun to set when I popped over the hill away from the fountain. I knew I was on limited time to find Zack because I had to be at a dinner with the aunts.

The sidewalk led to a quiet stretch of beach, where the water on the horizon shimmered with a vibrant white glow.

I looked back at my surroundings and noticed the illumination on the sandy cliffs. Just over that was the small Village.

"Wow." I stood at the base of the cliffs and noticed the rocky reef gradually exposed by the retreating tide.

Soon darkness would begin to fall since we still hadn't had daylight savings time. Seagulls and sandpipers brought me back to my main purpose. Find Zack.

Too bad I wouldn't be here long enough to soak in the last glimmers of daylight, I thought to myself as I took in the beautiful hillside views and the sound of the ocean as it met the shore.

I headed down the sidewalk along the street, where there were a few shops, before I slipped into a small bar called Happy Birthday Bar.

The name made me smile as it, too, went along with what seemed to be the theme around here.

The bar looked as if it were an old gas station. The large garage-style doors were pushed up and let the breeze off the sea float in and the music on the jukebox flow out.

There was the sound of laughter and chatter from people oblivious to what was going on over the hill behind them, or they just didn't care.

"Hey, you!" A familiar voice I recognized, Cherise, called out to me when I stepped through the garage door.

I looked up, scanning the tops of heads to find her. She was sitting at the far end of the bar, waving me over.

Along the way, I stopped to look at the photos on the wall. They were of patrons of the bar, who wore the paper cone birthday hats, with a shot glass with a lit candle inside lifted up next to the smiling faces.

"Fancy seeing you here." I sat down on the empty stool next to her and plopped my purse on top of the counter. "I thought you'd be at the big fountain ceremony."

"Nope. My people are right here." She picked up the shot glass and pushed it around in the air before she flung the liquid into her mouth. "Happy birthday!"

"Happy birthday!" the patrons of the bar shouted back.

"It's your birthday?" I asked.

"No." She cackled. "But someone has a birthday today, so we celebrate here. Do you want it to be your birthday? You get a birthday hat, song, and a photo for the wall."

"No. I'm good. Not much of a drinker," I told her.

"Oh, I beg to differ. You beat Fern in the beer competition," she reminded me.

"That was a rare occasion," I confessed.

"So you were trying to impress the most eligible bachelor in Holiday Junction, Rhett Strickland?" She had a little slur to her speech, making me wonder how long she'd been at the Happy Birthday Bar.

"Most eligible bachelor? What makes an airport security guard with a rooster as his boss so eligible?" I asked.

She flung her head forward, and her eyes shot up, looking at me from underneath her brows.

With the shot glass still in her hand, she pointed her finger at me.

"Are you telling me that you being the big-time investigative reporter you are had no idea Rhett Strickland is the richest man in the Village? He owns a lot of property."

"Are you sure we are talking about the same Rhett Strickland?" I questioned.

"What can I get you?" the bartender yelled over the music at me. I waved him off.

"Oh yeah. Me and Rhett go way back, until I cheated on him with his brother Patrick, who doesn't have a pot to piss in." She laughed out loud before she chased that shot with a swig of green beer.

"You what?" I put my hand in the air and waved to the bartender, pointing at the green beer Cherise had and indicating to get me one.

"Thatagirl." Her words slurred together.

"When in Rome." I shrugged, knowing I needed to pump her for more information, and from what I'd seen here in Holiday Junction, being part of the group was how I was going to get information I needed.

"Oh yeah, he owns most of the rental property. Like all of it." She held up her beer stein for me to clink for a cheers after the bartender slid mine down the bar, spilling most of it on its journey.

"Does he own Leni's sewing shop out near the countryside?" I asked.

"Mmmhhhmm," she ho-hummed.

"And you said you cheated on him with his brother?" I had to hit each bullet point one at a time as I pieced together my interactions I'd had with Rhett.

No wonder Leni had given him that piece of paper. I wondered why he didn't tell me who he was and found it interesting.

"Yep. Patrick is the black sheep of the family. He was exiled away from them a long time ago and didn't get a dime when none of them died. He does talk to the aunts but not Matthew." She rolled her eyes. "Patrick is my soul mate." She tapped her chest.

"He talks to Rhett though, right?" I asked because Rhett had told me what a great band Patrick's band was and how I had to go to the concert during the festival before we saw Cherise there.

"Yep. They are really tight. Don't let anyone fool you." She giggled. "I work a lot, so it's easy for the brothers to get along."

"Are you telling me Rhett still has a thing for you, and that's why he didn't want to stay around to listen to Patrick's band?" I asked.

"Look at you all inquiring-minds-want-to-know. You have a thing for him, don't you?" She smirked.

"No. Not a thing. I'm out of here on your first flight out, remember?" I knew she wouldn't remember any of this conversation.

"I remember. I also know the look of a Rhett Strickland lovesick woman, and my dear, I hate to tell you, but you've got that look." She got so close to my face our noses almost touched. "The look on Fern's face. That's the look on your face, so when you beat Fern in the beer competition, it was like you beat her in the Rhett competition, which is way more important to her. Wait until you meet the aunts. You think Fern is rough—they are brutal."

"I have met them, and let's say that they gave me some information to help me get out of here before my birthday, which is a few months away." I added the last part so she didn't signal to the bar that it was my birthday.

I opened my purse and pulled out the file Louise and Marge had given me along with the *Junction Journal*.

"Oh goodness, they've got that old rag still out. They need to drag that thing out into their mansion's backyard and shoot it. Put it out of its misery." She made me smile.

"I'm not saying you're wrong, but I do know I made an agreement with them for this file." I wagged it at her.

"Let's look." She grabbed it. "Shall we?" And she opened it. "Looks like they are doing their own little investigation. Here is the flight list."

"I asked Chief Strickland for that." I looked at the list along with Cherise.

"He is going to give it to his sister and wife before you," she said and drank the last of her beer.

"Sister and wife?" I wasn't sure I was following her.

"His wife is Aunt Marge." She put an emphasis on the name. "She's the worse one of the two aunts. Very judgy."

It was another thing Rhett Strickland hadn't told me. He wasn't obligated to tell me anything, but you'd think he'd introduce her by telling me she was Chief Strickland's wife.

No wonder they needed me to investigate. It would be a conflict of interest if she stuck her nose into the information. I'd been had by the aunts, and I felt the sting.

"You know, I shouldn't be telling you this, and maybe it's the liquid courage, but I should be fired for what happened to Jay Mann." She downed the beer.

Cherise and the bartender must've had some sort of agreement, because he continued to give her a new green beer after she'd finished the last.

"Why?" I looked down the passenger list and noticed Jay's name wasn't on it.

"I didn't clear the airplane before taking off. Something Jim Dixon checks off his list. As the head flight attendant, I'm supposed to go through the cabin every morning, every night, and between flights to make sure everyone was gone. I didn't do that, so I'm not even sure how long Jay's body had been there. But if you go back to the flight documents, I verbally told Jim I did these activities. So here I sit drowning my sorrows as I try to figure out how I tell the NTSB my story now that I heard they've been called in." Her words left me with my jaw dropped wide open.

She had referred to the National Transportation Safety Board, which would look at the flight now that there was a death. But if the death was nicely packaged up and solved, they would take that and close the case.

"If the NTSB gets here before the murder is solved, it could be weeks before I can leave." Worry lines increased on my forehead as my heartbeat quickened. "I've got to find Zack Hume and get an interview with Melissa Mann. I need to find out why Jay was on the plane and not on the list."

"Who knows." She shrugged. "Zack. He's right over there." She snorted a burp, and my eyes followed her finger over to the corner of the bar, way far away from the doors, to a silhouette in the corner. "I can get you an interview with Melissa. Sandra and I were best friends growing up. She moved, but we still keep in touch. She's in here, you know. Sad."

"Just how can you get me an interview?" I asked.

"I'll call," she said.

"You won't even remember this conversation," I told her.

"Yes, I will." She crisscrossed her fingers on her chest. "I feel bad for the Manns. They were so happy to tell their story about how they met when Melissa worked at the city clerk in the driver's license department as a teenager. Jay came in at sixteen to get his license, and that's how they met. Cute, right?"

"Wow, they've been together a long time." I knew this was a great love story to add to the article. Give Jay a little personal touch with family and love, which led to love of Holiday Junction and serving on the Hibernian board.

"Sandra was the cake, and Dana was the icing on their love story." Cherise sighed. "Something all of us want."

Cherise's mood had turned south, and I didn't want to be part of it. I needed to keep my head on straight, and that meant I had to talk to Zack.

"If you'll excuse me, I am going to go talk to Zack. Don't forget to get me that interview with Melissa Mann." I gathered the contents of the file and picked up the nearly full beer so I wouldn't look so out of place and headed over to Zack's table in the dark corner.

"I'm not interested." He greeted me with cold eyes.

"I'm not either." I sat down. "I'm with the *Junction Journal* and the *National News*."

He looked up at me.

"You're that reporter." He recognized me and shook his finger my way. "Aren't you? I can't tell much without all the black on your face."

"Not my finest moment finding a dead body, but hey, you can tell I had some emotions, which is why I came here to see you." I set the beer and the file on top of the table. "I'm looking into Jay Mann's case and now your wife's. I would appreciate anything you could tell me so we can bring her killer to justice."

His finger circled the rim of the beer mug, and his chin moved back and forth as though he was thinking about what I was saying.

"What do you want to know? She was a good wife. She was loyal even when it was hard for her to be." He sounded a little bitter. I sat and listened, careful not to interrupt him so he wouldn't stop talking. "She was proud to be in the women's part of the Hibernians as well as Jay Mann's loyal secretary..." His words fell off.

"Do you think she was murdered because she knew something about Jay Mann?" I asked.

"Seems like it, but I don't know why. I'm just blessed she gave me the last fifteen years. I chased her fifteen years before that." He smiled at the fond memory.

"I'm sorry. I really am. But do you know anyone who might've had motive?" I asked.

"No one. Rosey didn't see eye to eye with Layla Camsen, but I don't think it was enough for Layla to kill her." He reminded me of Layla's gardener.

"Again, I'm sorry for your loss." I gathered my things and walked back over to Cherise. "Do you know where I can find Reed Schwindt?"

"The Village maintenance man?" She leaned back with a curious snarl curled on her nose. "The odd-job guy?"

"That's him," I confirmed. "What do you know about him?"

"He did a lot of odd jobs for the Hibernian members at their homes." Her brows shot up. "But that's not a reason to kill somebody. About a week ago I was in here and he came in asking if there were any jobs that needed doing around the bar because he'd gotten fired from the society."

"Really?" I found that to be interesting. "He also did some work for the airport too."

"Yep. He is creepy with the old wooden cart he pushes around, and all those knives he sharpens gives me the heebie-jeebies." She shook.

"Do you know where I can find him?" I knew what Cherise told me gave him motive to have killed anyone who fired him, because it impacted his livelihood. Plus there were several accounts of hearing his squeaky cart.

"He's probably down at the jiggle joint about this time." She looked at her bare wrist as if there were a watch there.

"Where's the jiggle joint?" I asked.

She laughed. "About two blocks thataway."

CHAPTER EIGHTEEN

"Jiggle joint," I repeated to myself over and over as I approached the two-block mark where Cherise had told me I could find Reed, the maintenance man.

He'd been fired recently by a few of the Hibernian members as their handyman, and one of them was Jay Mann, the first victim. His murder seemed to be related to the second victim's murder.

It was also brought to my attention how he pushed a cart around the Village and kept knives, and I'm not talking dull knives either. From what I'd heard, he'd kept them nice and sharp.

"High-end gentleman's club?" I read a sign that pointed down an alleyway. My jaw dropped. "Jiggle joint." I shook my head at how naive I was for not realizing Cherise was talking about some sort of strip club.

I'd never in my life been to one of these, and I sure didn't know what to expect.

"It's for the good of your career, Violet," I told myself. "Buck up, girl. California is probably worse than this."

I didn't know anything about California other than they seemed to have a lot of big cities, forward-moving fashion trends, and really rich people. I'd seen photos all the time in the gossip papers with all the celebrities in their fancy homes and even the club with the bunny suits, so what was the big deal? I might'swell get my feet wet now so when I did have to do some big investigative work, I'd be prepared.

Yep. That's what I told myself right before I opened the door.

The stench of hot stuffy air and stagnant beer mixed with cheap cologne, hairspray, and smoke hit me as soon as I swung the door open. I sucked in a deep breath and held it once I walked in.

There was no way I could last in here more than two minutes. Okay, ten tops.

The strobe lights flickered to the beat of the overly loud music. There were shadowy silhouettes of a few patrons sitting around the stage at small round tables, watching the moon-shaped stage where there were two poles floor to ceiling.

Apparently that's where the talent performed. It must've been between acts because the stage was empty and the waitstaff was walking around with trays, taking orders.

"Honey, we aren't hiring," the bartender yelled at me.

"I'm not looking for a job," I told him and pulled out one of my old business cards from my purse. "I'm looking for Reed Schwindt."

"What? He stiff you on a job?" The bartender wiped down the counter, making me a clean spot to put my bag.

"No." I handed him the card.

He tilted it to the side for what little bit of light was in the place to hit it so he could read it.

A huge grin crossed his lips.

"You're that reporter. Honey, I sure didn't recognize you, but if you want a job, you got it. People are talking all about you, and, well, they'd pay to come see you." He slid my card next to the vodka bottle. "Can I get you a drink? On the house."

"No, thank you. I don't drink." I leaned in closer so I could talk to him without screaming over the MC, who was introducing the next talent.

"You don't?" He reached underneath the bar and pulled out the *Junction Journal*. "According to the journal, you sure did drink Fern under the table."

"That was a rare occasion." I glared at him and tried to take the paper, but he obviously anticipated my move, grabbing it before I could.

"What do you want then?" He leaned over, and his breath smelled of beer. "With Reed?"

"I am doing an investigation piece for the *Junction Journal*." I could see the hesitation on his face. "I know. Why would I help a paper who clearly railroaded me?" I nodded to the paper in his hands. "Anyways, I am working with them while I'm here. A reporter such as myself can't stop the tickle of the investigation just because I'm stuck here. I decided to take them up on their offer for me to join them."

"Is that right?" The right side of his lip curled. "I'll be right back."

He moved down the bar, leaving me alone with a couple of patrons at the bar, huddled over their drinks with their eyes on me.

"Good show tonight," I told them, lifting my chin to the stage and looking over my shoulder to see exactly what was going on. I didn't care for what I saw, so I turned back to the bar.

"Say, aren't you that reporter?" one of the men asked.

"Violet Rhinehammer." I took the opportunity to introduce myself since I could see the bartender using his cell phone. No doubt checking out my story. "I'm doing an exposé on the murders here in Holiday Junction, and I'd love for you to give me a statement concerning the two victims, Jay Mann and Rosey Hume. And if you know of anyone who had motive to kill them?"

"Nah." The one man slowly shook his head and looked at the other guy.

"Nope. I bet Jay did something to someone, and since Rosey was his secretary, she knew some secrets that someone didn't want out. Like you southerners say, sweep it under the rug." He eased the beer mug up to his lips and took a sip.

"How did you know I'm southern?" I asked.

"Honey, you're a stranger around here. Holiday Junction might be a little bit bigger city than where you're from, but the gossip isn't different. My wife told me all about you before you left the airport that day with Rhett Strickland."

My gut stung with a little bit of shock when I realized that everyone in Holiday Junction knew every single thing about me.

"Speaking of the Stricklands. I'm working for the *Junction Journal* while I'm stuck here, so I'm using my keen investigating skills to find the killer." I said it with pride and confidence. "I'm actually here looking for Reed."

"He was here and fixed the sign, but he's gone now."

"What's your name?" I asked, taking my notepad out of my purse.

"The Easter Bunny." He elbowed his friend.

"Let me guess," I said to the other one. "You're Santa Claus."

"Me?" He snickered and swiveled his back to me. "Can't you see my wings? I'm the tooth fairy."

Both men got a big kick out of making fun of me.

"Owen. Shawn." The bartender had rejoined us. "Are you giving our new reporter a hard time?"

"I was just about to ask her what she wanted in her Easter basket." The man who claimed he was the Easter bunny had a huge grin on his face.

"Owen, that's not nice. Apologize to the lady." The bartender gave him a stern look then shifted his eyes to the beer.

"Fine. I'm sorry. Welcome to Holiday Junction," he said before he muttered under his breath, "I'm only sorry because Darren won't give me another beer."

"Darren?" My ears had perked, as had my brows. I looked at the bartender. "Well, Darren, did the sisters of the *Junction Journal* confirm my identity?"

"They sure did. Darren Strickland. Nephew to the family. You've created quite the stir in our happy clan." Now that I took a good look at him, there was a slight resemblance to Rhett. "I understand my cousin, Rhett, has been awfully kind to you."

"I think he wants the killer to be found just as much as I do. Which brings me to why I'm here." I flipped the page in the notebook in hopes of getting some real information about Reed.

"She's asking for Reed," Shawn said and stood up, dropping a couple of bucks on the counter.

"It's my understanding he'd be here." I wrote down the names of Owen, Shawn, and cousin Darren, just so it would look like I was really writing something down.

"You think Reed had something to do with the murders?" Darren asked, put a stein under the spout of a beer tap, and pulled it to fill it up. He placed it on a tray and filled up two more so the waitstaff could come get the order.

"From what I hear, he was fired recently and has a motive. Not only that, but he also has a lot of knives, and both victims were killed with a knife." I flipped the empty notebook pages back and forth like I was reading from them.

I was really playing the part, and I could tell he was trying to see what I had written down.

"A couple of eyewitnesses recalled hearing squeaky wheels coming from the fountain about the time of Rosey Hume's murder. I'd like to talk to him about that. Do you know where I can find him?" I put my pen to the notebook.

"You tell me where I can find some of that invisible ink." Darren knew I didn't have anything written down. "And I'll give you all the information I know."

"Fine." I shoved the notebook back in my purse, giving up the professional act. "You seem like a hardworking, decent guy. I'm only trying to help out your uncle, Chief Strickland. He asked me to help, and you know what? I have nothing to do, so I'm just trying to keep busy until I can leave."

"Honesty. I like that in a person." He paused as though he was thinking about what to say to me.

"Thank you." I smiled, giving him a minute to get his thoughts together. "I do appreciate any help you can offer me. I know in a place like this you hear a lot. Especially from men who have loose lips after drinking. I'm sure your uncle has already asked you if you heard anything."

"No. He only goes by the book, and he'd never even think about using common sense to get some clues." His demeanor softened. "Reed didn't do it. I would bet my jiggle joint on it."

His grin was infectious and made me grin.

"That's what Cherise called it, right?" he asked, even though I didn't have to answer because he knew. "What about Vern McKenna? He and Reed are pretty tight, and from what I understand, they've been seen together at all hours of the day and night. But I know Reed. There's no way he did it. Plus Vern has access to Reed's cart, and yeah, it does squeak. Reed told me once after I asked if I could grease up the wheels how he liked them squeaking so people could hear him coming. Now, if he were going to kill someone, he's smart enough to leave that cart behind. Have you checked out Vern's secret shed in the woods behind Leni's sewing shop?"

"Nope. I didn't even know about it."

"Rhett didn't tell you?" He scoffed.

"No. He didn't." I wondered why he didn't tell me or even point it out when we were at the shop. "He doesn't tell me a lot of things."

"I bet he left out the part where he applied to the Hibernian Society and they denied him." That was some news to chew on.

"Let me guess, Jay Mann was the president?" I knew the answer since Jay had been the president for a long time.

"Bingo." He gave me the handgun movement with his hand, indicating I was right on target. "And Jay Mann refused to let Sandra go out with him. He's not a fan of Jay Mann's."

I wasn't sure, but I really did feel like Darren was selling me the possibility Rhett Strickland should be looked at as a suspect.

"Vern and Rhett are tight." He crossed his fingers. "Like father-and-son tight."

"And Vern was just named Hibernian president." My thought shifted back to how happy Leni was to see Rhett and then the list of items she needed done for the shop.

"Vern is also his godfather. See the connection with Reed?" he asked.

The ringing phone took his attention from our conversation.

I flipped the notepad and started to scribble down the entwined relationships between Vern, Reed, and Rhett. Rhett had been burned in the past by Jay Mann because Jay wouldn't let Sandra go out with Rhett. Then Rhett's father had died, which I had no idea how, but it didn't matter. Vern was Rhett's godfather and wanted to see Rhett succeed.

But according to Cherise, Rhett had so much money he didn't know what to do with it. Money didn't give someone busy time, which was why Rhett wanted to be in the Hibernians, but Jay shot it down. Not only that, with Jay out of the way, Vern would be appointed as president, where he could approve Rhett for membership.

And if Vern and Reed were as tight as Darren claimed, it would be easy for Vern to have access to the cart so people would hear it. The nosy people who would recognize the sound would hear it.

This would be premeditated murder.

My mind was going faster than my hand could write.

Vern would also know that Reed was fired from doing work around Jay Mann's house, and I couldn't help but wonder if Rosey did know too much, making her the last victim so Vern could go through with his plan for his godson?

I tapped the head of the pen on the notebook and knew it was time I find that shed of Vern McKenna's.

After flipping the notebook shut, I threw it and the ink pen down into my bag.

If I timed it right, I could take the path along the wooded area back and check out the shed before I headed back in time for supper at the aunts'.

There I knew I could confront Rhett in front of his uncle and get him arrested right then and there.

"Violet!" I heard Darren call my name just as I reached for the door handle. I turned around. He had the phone cradled between his shoulder and ear. "Chief Strickland is my dad."

CHAPTER NINETEEN

There seemed to be a lot more depth to the Strickland family than I knew or even cared to know about. If I were living here, I might've tried to dig deeper into why these men all seemed to have some sort of family issues. There was some deep sort of feeling there, but I had no time to figure any of that out.

If Darren was right and Vern was the suspect his father should look at, then I was going to go there right now and get the answers so I could be out of here on the first flight in the morning.

When I looked away from the seaside, the mountainous background surrounded Holiday Junction. If my memory was correct, the fountain was the opposite way from Leni's shop, and the wooded country area would be toward the right.

Just past the seaside shops, which were your typical little hobby shops for tourists, was where the land gave way to sandy streets with small cottage houses.

I decided to walk down one going away from the sea and toward the mountains. Though I was in a little bit of a hurry since I was already going to be late for dinner, I still took in the scenery and noticed all the cute clapboard houses that lined each side of the street.

The sound of gentle waves lapping against the beach was behind me.

Each cottage home was painted a different vibrant color. Many had boats or motorized water vehicles parked under a car porch, along with a segment of chain-link fence to divide the properties.

With each step, I thought of how nice it must be to live in Holiday Junction with what seemed like the perfect setting to live, where you could pop over the hill and get a healthy dose of sun, sand, and seaside bliss.

My arrival as I passed along the houses was met with some barks and some stares from the homeowners, but mostly with a wave and friendly smile.

Holiday Junction was honestly pure charm. Too bad the murders were looming over such a festive time here.

At the end of the sandy street was a rickety bridge built out of boards. Clearly the salty conditions had taken a toll on it, as seen from the rusty nails popping up. I took one last look back and knew time was slipping past as the sun was starting to kiss the edge of the ocean.

I hurried down the sandy path and noticed each step of the way, the walkway started to turn into more grass and clay, taking me deeper and deeper into the woods.

I jerked my head when I heard a bark. I stopped to listen. It was definitely Monty, Layla Camsen's dog, which told me I was near their home. That meant I was near Leni's sewing shop. The building and land Rhett Strickland owned.

I whistled out to keep Monty barking. He would lead me right to the area I needed to be in order to find the shed. Darren said it was located on Rhett's property that Leni rented, and it did make sense because she was married to Vern.

Just like I knew he would, Monty continued to bark as I headed his way through the thick of the woods along the beaten path. I wasn't sure if it was a path made by woodland animals, but from the continued marks that resembled the marks of wheels, I could only come to the conclusion this was the path Reed took while pushing his cart.

The path reminded me of my home in Normal, Kentucky, which

was located in the Daniel Boone National Forest. We had thousands of trails just like this, and it was kind of nice to feel safe for a moment.

The snap of a dried branch brought me out of my thoughts. I looked ahead and saw a small shed-like building with a tall, lanky man with thinning hair walking out of the shed. When he turned around, I recognized him as Vern McKenna from the Greening of the Fountain ceremony.

I jumped behind a large oak, placing my back against it in hopes Vern had not heard me. His footsteps were going away from me, which calmed my breathing a little more, and when I heard a car door slam, I knew I was in the clear for the moment.

When I leaned around the tree, the shed was on a beeline in front of me, and Monty was barking to the left of me.

"Good boy, Monty," I whispered for him to hear me when I hurried down the path to the shed. "You did a good job."

Monty's ears perked up, and he moved on to smelling something.

I opened the door to the shed and was met with the odor of paint. The opened spray cans littered the ground. As the last bit of sunlight filtered through the door, my eyes scanned up past the paint, and there was a large piece of wood cut out in the form of an Easter basket filled with lilies.

Suddenly a shadow draped the inside. I jumped around.

"What are you doing here? Who are you?" Vern stood at the door of the shed. "You." He wagged a finger. "You're that reporter."

"And I'm here to get answers about the real truth behind Jay Mann and Rosey Hume and your hand in their deaths." I took a step back when he stalked inside.

His hands were covered in paint. He drew a handkerchief from his back pocket and began to wipe them.

"What kind of investigative reporter are you?" He shook his head. "I have no reason or motive to have killed either of them."

"Then you can answer a few questions for me." Nervously I fiddled with my purse and dug down to get my notepad and pen. "I understand you were seen with the two of them. I also know you are Rhett Strickland's godfather, who would do anything for him, which is pretty convenient seeing how Rhett was denied membership to the Hibernian Society under Jay's presidency."

"You honestly think Rhett cares enough about the society to become a member that we'd have to kill someone to make it happen?" Vern continued to shake his head like a disappointed father. "I don't think so."

"How do you explain being with Rosey and Jay at night?" I asked.

"Because I am the Merry Maker, and Jay was going to take over for me."

My face scrunched up. "The Merry Maker?"

"Lucky Leprechaun, Father Time, Mother's Day Basket." He pointed to the large wooden basket.

"You are the secret person who puts out the big figures and picks the neighborhood." I remembered Rhett telling me about it.

"Yes. I'm getting older, and I simply can't continue to carry these around and at night. I've gotten Reed to help me out a lot, but Jay is— was much younger than me. He was going to take over, like I said. A few days ago, he told me he wasn't going to be able to commit to it because Dana was sick and he wasn't sure he'd even be here during all the holidays. Rosey said that she would do it and get her husband to help her."

"So you were showing them the ropes?" I asked.

"Yes. I didn't feel comfortable with it being just me and Rosey. I asked Reed to come, but he wasn't able to because he was doing some work for the police department that night." Vern walked past me, picked up a bottle of white spray paint off the floor, and painted another lily.

"That's why the police department hasn't arrested Reed, because he has an alibi." I wondered why Chief Strickland hadn't told me this little bit of information.

"Unfortunately, I'm going to have to go to the police now that you are here. They must think I killed Jay and Rosey." He threw the spray can down. "I guess I don't have to finish this because everyone will know I'm the guy." He laughed. "Leave it to me to break this hundred-year-old tradition for Holiday Junction. Leni is going to kill me."

I looked back at the big basket for Mother's Day and sighed.

"Chief Strickland hasn't mentioned to me that you're a suspect. I've been gathering leads and, well, the squeaky wheel of Reed's cart led me to information about you. Now you're telling me Reed was at the police station working, so that eliminates him as well." I flipped through my notes. "Darren sure did have my wheels turning."

"Darren Strickland?" Vern laughed. "My first words of advice are not to trust anything that comes out of Darren Strickland's mouth."

"Funny. He said the same thing about you." Not really in those words, but as he talked about Rhett, I could tell Darren didn't trust Rhett or Vern.

Again, something ran deep between Rhett and Darren, but I didn't care. I was too busy trying to get myself out of here. Not solve some family tiff.

"Speaking of the Stricklands." I shoved the notebook back in my purse, feeling a little defeated. "I've got to go. I was invited to supper by the aunts."

"Interesting. I've known them all my life—as you know, I'm Rhett's godfather—and I've never been invited for dinner." He made it sound like I was special. "You must be special."

I cackled out loud. "You've got to be kidding me. They don't want me around. Have you ever heard keep our friends close but keep enemies closer?" There was an eerie pause between us.

"What are you thinking?" Vern asked.

"I'm thinking I'm on to something the Stricklands don't want me to know." I gripped the straps of my purse, knowing the aunts had given me the file, and wondered if it was just a wild-goose chase they were sending me on.

"It wouldn't be the first reporter the aunts got rid of." His words sent chills down my back.

CHAPTER TWENTY

It was all set in my head when I left Vern at the shed to finish up the upcoming Merry Maker's secret job that I was going to head straight over to the Strickland mansion and confront the aunts about what they were hiding.

The one thing I knew was that none of the young men in the family got along at all. Patrick and Rhett were at odds due to Cherise, or so it seemed. Darren and Rhett, well, heck, I had no idea why they didn't get along. The two instances had one person in common.

Rhett Strickland.

Though Vern said that he didn't kill Jay and Rosey, he sure didn't exonerate Rhett Strickland himself. Even Cherise had said it—Rhett was the most eligible bachelor. Rhett sure was keeping tabs on me.

Who did he think he was? I was smarter than that. I was Violet Rhinehammer, *National News* correspondent, and the little attention he was giving me wasn't going to get me off track. If anything, it put me on high alert. Which also begged the question of whether Chief Strickland was on the up-and-up.

It wasn't common but also not unheard of for people in authority to do things to cover up something for a family member. Sending a fine investigative reporter like myself on a wild-goose chase would be a way to keep me busy running around Holiday Junction, knowing I was going to hit a dead end.

Then the aunts gave me this useless file?

My phone rang. I continued to walk and pulled my phone out from my bag.

"Hello?" I didn't recognize the number.

"Is this Violet Rhinehammer, *the* big-time investigative reporter?" Cherise cackled from the other end of the phone in her drunken-stupor voice, emphasizing a couple of words to mock me.

"Funny, Cherise." I stopped so I could concentrate now more than ever. "Did you get me that interview?"

I still wanted to talk to Melissa Mann and get her take on who she thought would want her husband dead.

"Sure did. Right now." Cherise rattled off the address. "They are at home now. Sandra said they were going to be busy the next few days getting the funeral arrangements ready for her dad, but you can go there now."

"Now?" My ear and shoulder hugged the phone while I took out my notepad to scribble down the Manns' address.

"Now or never." Cherise hiccupped. "And this will make you happy."

"What's that?" I asked.

"The NTSB cleared us for takeoff tomorrow night, so it seems like you're out of here." She hiccupped again. "That means I've got to call Patrick to come get me so I can get to bed."

"Really?" My heart raced, and for a second I thought about not going to see the Manns or going to the Strickland supper, but the little investigative reporter told me I had to find out what I could so I could report back to Richard Stone, who had yet to call me back from all of my voicemails I'd left him.

I wasn't too worried about him not getting in touch with me. He knew I was stuck here and working hard. He had to have been doing some investigating on his end too.

"That's great news, Cherise. Thank you!" I looked at the notebook where I'd written down the address. "I'll see you on the airplane tomorrow!"

She mumbled a few things before the phone went silent.

Quickly I pulled up the map app on my phone and plugged in the Manns' address. The Stricklands were going to have to wait. Their little wild-goose chase they'd sent me on was going to be a joke on them. I was going to find something out. Something of importance, and I was sure Melissa or Sandra Mann would be able to give me some names.

"Richard, thank goodness I got in touch with you." I couldn't believe Richard answered my call on my walk over to the Manns' house, which according to the map was about a mile away.

At first glance I groaned at the walk, but now that he had answered, I picked up the pace and got a new breath of life.

"Good news. The NTSB has cleared our flight to leave tomorrow, so I should be in your office as soon as I get off the airplane." I would find out later if I was going to be sending a car for me, which was the least of my worries. "I've got some very interesting information."

I told him all about the Stricklands and the *Junction Journal* as well as all the leads that'd turned up empty or just didn't end in enough evidence to peg someone as a killer.

"Right now Jay Mann's widow and daughter are expecting me. I'm on my way there now to interview them, but honestly, I want to know who they think killed Jay. What do you think?" I asked.

"I think you need to stop the investigation on who killed Jay Mann and get the down low on the Strickland family. There's a lot of history there." Richard knocked me for a loop. "From the information we've uncovered, the founding fathers of Holiday Junction were Stricklands. The brothers had actually dueled each other to be the first mayor, and they both ended up dead."

"No wonder the mayor is a dog," I muttered and looked down at my phone when it beeped for me to take a right down the next street. "But I don't care about the Stricklands. I wanted to do the piece on the murders and continue my coverage for when I get there."

"I'm sorry, Violet, but as the editor in chief of the paper, I need to see all of your skills, and one of those is taking orders. If you can't pass that part of the interview, then you can just board the airplane back to Kentucky." His words stung, but I knew it was tough love to let me know that I'd made it to the big time.

"Besides, I've got our best investigative reporter headed to Holiday Junction tonight to start our live broadcasts with a real cameraman and crew."

"Great! I'm really excited to have the opportunity to get in front of the camera. When do they get here?" I asked.

"I don't think you understand, Violet. You're not going to be broadcasting anything. You can give our team all of your information, and we will see you for your interview tomorrow." He finished up with "Thanks, Violet, for your work" before he hung up.

My blood was boiling. It took everything in my body to resist calling up my parents, tucking tail, and doing exactly what Richard Stone said—hightail it back to Kentucky.

Then I couldn't help but wonder if he was pulling my leg. Was he really trying to see what I was made of? A team player?

"Yeah. A team player." I nodded and stopped right in front of the house that my map had pinpointed to be the Mann house.

The idea of Richard Stone testing me really got me excited. I was up for the challenge, and with Sandra's and Melissa Mann's thoughts on who they thought did this horrific act, I knew I would find the killer. Not only that, but I was so geared up to prove the Stricklands and the aunts wrong about me that nothing at this point was going to stop me. Not even the deep excitement about me boarding a plane to my dreams tomorrow.

The Mann home was exactly how I thought it was going to be ever since I saw his fancy silk square. It was the typical two-story brick home that looked modest on the outside and like it was built on a couple of acres. The houses in their neighborhood weren't too close together but not too far apart.

"You must be the reporter." A woman who looked to be my age opened the door after I'd rung the doorbell.

"Yes. Violet Rhinehammer." I handed her one of my old Channel Two business cards because it was all I had to prove my job. "I'm sorry to hear about your dad."

"Thank you." She looked at my business card. She waved me to follow her.

The inside had many pieces of expensive furniture that screamed they had money.

"I'm Sandra."

"Is your mom going to be okay?" I asked Sandra and followed her into their family room, where she gestured for me to sit on the couch.

"I'm not sure. I definitely won't go back home until she is. My husband and I will make it work. I'm so glad Mom got to spend some time with Dad at my house. I'm grateful Dad forgot his wallet at my house the night he flew out, because Mom said he embraced her and told her how happy he was with our family and life."

My heart ached for their loss. That the love was strong between them was apparent from how they spoke of each other.

"Are you two talking about me?" Melissa walked in on my and Sandra's conversation. "I'm going to be fine. It'll take time, but I hope with all the attention you are giving his murder, they will find the person who did this."

"I'm not sure if you heard, but there's been a second victim. Rosey Hume," I said.

"No! Not Rosey!" She buried her head in her hands. Sandra rushed over to her mom's side. "Who is doing this? Why?"

"I'm hoping you can shed some light on some questions that hopefully the killer will see in my piece." I left out the part that I was going to write it up in the *Junction Journal* as my part to keep good on my word to the aunts.

"Nana!" Jay and Melissa's granddaughter rushed into the room. "Mommy said I have to take off my dress."

"We don't want to ruin it." Sandra came back into the room.

"She won't. I'll buy a new one, two, or three for my little Dana."

Melissa bent down and hugged her granddaughter. She slid her hand down the back of the little girl's hair.

"Careful or you'll pull out my tube." The little girl pulled out of the big hug.

"We can't have that now, can we?" Melissa reached for the little girl's hand. "I love you."

"I love you." Dana turned around and looked up at her mom. "See. Nana said she'd buy me another one."

Sandra looked at her mom and shook her head.

"Why weren't you like this when I was a kid?" she teased her mom and picked Dana up.

"I think parents are like that with their grandchildren." I smiled. "Can I get a photo of you two before I leave? For the article?"

"Of course." Sandra snugged Dana a little closer. "Smile."

I used my phone to snap a photo before they left the room.

"I thought it would be nice for you to see Jay for what he loved, not how you found him." Her eyes softened. "I can see you're shocked I know that you were the one who found him."

"I didn't know you knew." I occupied myself with taking my notebook out of my bag so I didn't have to look into her sad eyes.

"I have a question for you." She touched me.

I stopped busying myself and looked at her.

"Did you see his eyes?"

That struck me as an odd question.

"No. His chin was tucked, and when I noticed the blood, I immediately turned to Cherise. You do know Cherise?"

"Of course. She has been here several times when she and Sandra were children. I've talked to her since Sandra, Dana, and I flew home early. Like you, she said that when she looked into the airplane bathroom, she didn't look at his face."

Cherise told her that she looked at him? She might've for a minute, but she didn't get his ID like they'd told me to do. There was no need to even bring that up.

"He has the kindest eyes." Melissa motioned for me to follow her out through the sliding glass doors that led to the backyard of the house. On the way, she grabbed a set of keys off a set of hooks close to the door. "When we first met, it was his eyes that made me fall head over heels in love."

"From what I gather, you two have been together for a very long time." I tried to walk behind her and write down things as she talked.

"We have. I think I chased him all over this Village." She stopped and let me catch up with her. "That's his man-cave out there." She laughed. "He could stay out there for hours. I had no idea what he was doing."

There was a small house-type shed in the back corner of their property that backed up to the woods.

Melissa fumbled with the keys in the lock. After trying a couple different ones, she got one to work and unlocked the shed door.

"As you can see, I hardly ever came in here, much less had the opportunity to unlock it." She felt around for the light switch, illuminating the inside, which I'd have called more of a workshop. "What happened to Rosey?"

"The same thing that happened to your husband, not really the same thing, but they were both, um." I bit my lip.

"Go on. I can take it," she sniffled.

"Both stabbed and they both had the same pocket square on them." It was starting to sound like I was the magnet for these murders. "I was looking for your gardener, Reed, because a few people have mentioned he pushed around a squeaky cart."

"What does that have to do with anything?" She blinked as if she were trying to put two and two together.

"People have heard squeaky wheels at Rosey Hume's crime scene. Plus he does the landscape for the airport." I knew I was laying out the motive for her. "And I understand Jay had recently fired him from doing your landscape. I was by the seaside and heard he walked through the woods."

There was no need for me to tell her it was a jiggle joint and how Jay had gone there a lot.

"You mean the people at the strip club told you?" She rolled her eyes.

"Those guys." She tsked. "They honestly had no idea we wives knew they were there. I guess it was nice when Jay went there because I received the benefits afterwards, if you know what I mean."

I skimmed over her observation because it kind of made me feel a little icky.

"Are you saying Reed killed my husband?" she asked.

"I'm not sure, but it does look like it was his knife. I'm not sure who killed him. I can't help but wonder if he was about to attack someone and they turned his knife on him, but I'm sure Chief Strickland will get it all worked out." I flipped the notepaper to a clean sheet. I didn't tell her the police claimed Reed had an alibi. "Why don't you tell me about these articles?"

I wanted to give her some time to think about what I'd just said, so I changed the subject to let her talk about something that was in her memory. It was a little technique we liked to use to get to know a victim's family so they'd open up about their loved ones, and it was truly magical how they would see the reporter as a friend and just open up.

There were a lot of framed photos and articles on the wall in the shed.

"He loved to cut articles out of the *Junction Journal* about the Hibernians. He was the youngest to be elected president of our chapter." She pointed to the frame with the photo of a young Jay with Melissa by his side.

"As you go down the wall, you can see the story of his life. These might be good to just hang up in the funeral home as his eulogy." She looked as proud as I would expect him to look if he was here to show me himself.

"Is that Sandra?" I pointed to the one with them holding a baby. Both of them were dressed up.

"Yes. That's when we brought her home from the hospital," she said, her voice breaking.

"You look great for just having a baby." I didn't mean for it to sound like it came out. "I'm sorry. I don't have children."

"I do look good there." It was her way of giving me a pass. "We adopted Sandra twenty-eight years ago."

I knew Sandra was my age.

Melissa looked at the photo of them holding the little baby.

"Adoption is a wonderful thing, but as you know, my granddaughter needs a kidney transplant. And, well, now I wish we'd known who the mother was so we could get the donation. Downside of adoption. Jay and I thought we were doing a great thing, but the heartache with my granddaughter is almost too much to bear. Now I have to go through it alone." She looked away and down at the floor.

"What do you do now?" I wondered about the granddaughter but was careful considering the sensitive subject matter. "For your grand-daughter?"

"We wait. That's all we can do. Just wait for a donor. You can see she has chronic kidney disease, and, well, she's a trooper." She tapped the photo. "Jay and I both hoped we could be donors, but neither of us could."

"What about Sandra and Dana's dad?" I asked.

"They aren't compatible either." She frowned. "DNA is a funny thing."

Melissa ran her finger over her husband's face before she broke down in tears, bringing her fingers to her wedding band before clutching them to her chest.

"I'm so sorry." I reached out and ran my hand over her arm. "I know I don't know you, but I'm sorry you have to go through this. It seems like one tragedy after another for you. It's a lot to take in."

"If it weren't for baby Dana, I'm not sure I could survive. At least I live another day to pray she'll get a donor and live a full life." She let go of a long sigh and wiped away the tears from her face. "Goodness. I need something to drink. Can I get you something to drink?" Melissa asked. "You can take some photos while I go grab us something refreshing."

"Sure. I'll have whatever you're having." I knew she needed a moment to herself so she could gather her thoughts for the interview.

I took some snapshots of the photos. It appeared to be Jay's trophy wall, the things he was most proud of. All of his life was there in frames. I could see him aging through the progression of the photos.

"Mom! Mom!" Sandra rushed into the shed. "Where's my mom?" she asked me after she looked around and saw me standing there alone.

"She went inside to get a drink." I noticed Sandra was excited. "Are you okay?"

"More than okay. Rosey Hume is a match for Dana!" she screamed out with a look of disbelief. "I had no idea she was a donor until the doctor just called and said we have to get to the hospital now. It's what we've been waiting for. Who knew? The donor was under our noses this entire time! I've got to find my mom!"

Sandra slammed the shed door behind her, making one of the photo frames fall off the wall, scattering the glass all over the floor.

I bent down to pick up the pieces and noticed a piece of paper had also fallen out with the photo. The photo was the one where Jay and Melissa were holding Sandra on the day she was born.

I unfolded the piece of paper and read the caption, "I know you'll be taken better care of by your daddy. I will always love you. Rosey."

"Rosey?" I reread the caption again. I glanced back at the photos along the wall. Jay's wall. Jay's photos. "Sandra is Rosey and Jay's daughter?"

The ice rattling in the glass of tea caught my attention. I looked up. Melissa was standing in the door with two glasses of tea.

"I'm sorry I didn't hear you come in." I gulped and stood up, looking the killer in the eyes.

"I was coming here to let you know I need to cut this interview short, but it looks like I'm going to have some business to attend to with you before I can go." She glided her foot across the floor and used the heel of her shoe to shut the door.

"So you took two lives for one," I said and pretended to write something down on the notepad in hopes my hunch was right. If it was, this would be the biggest story of my life.

"Excuse me, you've got it wrong. Three." She reached up to another photo, the photo where Jay had been anointed as the president, and took the frame off the wall. "Jay, Rosey, and you."

The sound of tape ripping crippled my instinct to run out of the shed as fast as I could, then she exposed a knife.

"You can just let me go now that Chief Strickland believes Reed murdered Jay and Rosey for firing him. Let me get on my airplane to California. I'll never think of this again. It's up to you." I tried to make a good compelling argument for her to let me go. "No one will ever know you are trying to frame Reed for the murders."

"I really wish I could do it, and when I checked you out, you didn't seem so smart." She snickered. A far cry from the tearstained face she'd had a short time ago. "Guess I was wrong."

"If you're going to kill me, let me take a stab at what happened." I was doing anything I could to buy me some time to try to think up some grand scheme for how to get around her without getting a knife stuck in my side.

"You don't have to guess. I'm more than happy to confess. Get it off my chest. Let you take it to the grave." She had this gross jovial laugh that caused her shoulders to shake to life. "It goes way back to when Rosey had her claws, her filthy, wrong-side-of-the-tracks claws into Jay. That's when she tried to take him away from me by seducing him. I can't have children, so she got pregnant on purpose, but I wasn't going to let him go."

"You're saying he had no hand in the affair?" I blurted out when my fear turned to anger when I realized Melissa had given him a pass all these years. "And you did the right thing by adopting Sandra?"

"Sandra was our daughter. Mine and Jay's." She held the knife down, scraping the fancy green dress against her leg with the sharp end. "Rosey was just the vessel for her to come to me."

"Why did you kill them?" I asked and kept my peripheral vision on the knife she was still dragging along the side of her leg. A red streak was forming on the fabric, which told me she had no idea she'd cut herself.

"All these years I ignored Rosey. No one knew she was the vessel carrying my daughter. When we found out she'd seduced Jay and became planted"—her choice of words let me know I was dealing with a wacko and I had to tread this situation lightly—"she had nothing. Jay wasn't going to leave me for her, so we told her we'd take care of the baby by adopting the baby and wouldn't ruin her name here in Holiday Junction. The only reason she was around was the deal we'd made. Of course Jay was able to stay friends with her, and I'm not so sure she wasn't blackmailing him, because recently I found them sneaking around at night."

I found it so interesting how delusional Melissa was about the affair. In her mind she felt like it was all Rosey's fault and somehow Rosey was carrying the baby for Melissa.

"Sneaking around? At night?" My jaw dropped. "You don't know."

"Don't know what?" She glared.

"Jay and Rosey helped Vern put out the Lucky Leprechaun." I hated to tell her the big secret identity, but she needed to be set straight. My words took the color right out of her face. "Rosey and her husband were happy. Jay loved you and your family."

"It doesn't matter. I knew she was the one who could help Dana since none of us were a match. I also knew she was an organ donor because she'd always picked the option on her license when we were younger and I had a job at the clerk's license office. Jay knew it too. He even asked her at the last meeting if she'd consider getting tested, and she refused. She was born with one kidney, so I took it. Jay told me not to do something crazy, and I knew I had to save Dana with or without him."

"But how did you kill Jay?" I had to know.

"Jay never kept track of his schedule. I told him his flight was that night, and I had a ticket as well, but I'm sure you followed up on how I didn't take the flight. I got on the flight, and like always, he goes to the bathroom before they close the door. It's a thing with him. I followed him into the bathroom, and that's when I killed him."

Two and two weren't adding up for me.

"How did you get a knife on board the airplane?" I knew if I could get out of here, this article would definitely be the final fork I needed in order to secure my job with Richard Stone.

"Easy. The same plane goes back and forth to our daughter's. You've seen how things work around here. I simply took Jim Dixon a home-made pie for being such a great pilot and walked into our airport, where Rhett Strickland let me walk right on in." She was so cunning. "Jim took the pie and walked into the cockpit while I sashayed my way down the aisle of the empty airplane, where I slipped this little knife in the paper towel holder in the bathroom. That way when I got on the flight that night with Jay, the knife was already on board."

"Mom!" The door swung open with force, hitting Melissa in the back. She was flung forward, dropping the knife so she could use her hands to catch herself.

The knife skidded across the shed floor.

Melissa and I scrambled, knocking each other out of the way to get the knife.

"Stand back!" I screamed at Melissa, waving the knife in front of me. "Sandra," I tried to talk to her calmly.

"Don't listen to her, Sandra. This woman is crazy. You are my daughter. Not Rosey's. Do you understand me?" Melissa pleaded with Sandra.

Sandra looked at me and back to Melissa. She looked at the photo and the piece of paper on the ground. She picked it up.

"Don't believe their lies! I am protecting you! You are mine! All mine!" Melissa sounded like a mad woman who'd do anything to keep her life going as it was.

"Mommy, did you tell Nana I'm going to live?" Dana stood at the door with the cute little dress on and a little suitcase in her grasp.

"Your real Nana saved your life." Sandra picked up Dana, put her on her hip, and headed up to the house. I was sure they were going straight to the hospital.

Melissa curled up into a ball. Sandra's words killed her more than me holding her at knifepoint, which made it easy for me to call Chief Strickland to come pick up the real killer.

CHAPTER TWENTY-ONE

"**W**hy don't you let me give you a ride over to the Lucky Leprechaun?" Matthew Strickland had offered to give me a ride to the Jubilee Inn after I'd given him my statement about what had happened.

They'd taken Melissa into custody and given Sandra and Dana a police escort to the hospital, where Sandra's birth mother had given the ultimate gift. Life to Dana by being the organ donor.

By the torn look on Sandra's face, I knew there was going to be a lot of healing going on in that family. I was almost happy she didn't live here in Holiday Junction, where I was sure everyone and everything would remind her of what had happened.

It was best she took Dana back after the surgery and lived a full life with her husband there.

"Nah. I better get back to the inn so I can get a good night's sleep since I'll be heading off to California in the morning." It was nice to offer, and I appreciated it, but I didn't need to go and see Rhett, nor did I care to find out what their big family secrets were all about.

There was no doubt the luck of the Irish was with me when I was in Jay Mann's shed. Plus I wanted to look my best when I showed up at Richard's office, where my dream job would be offered to me.

"Oh, come on. Everyone will want to congratulate you on finding the real killer." He glanced over at me from the driver's side. "You did some real good work for an amateur."

"I'll have you know that I'm a real investigative reporter," I snapped back and knew I still had something to prove before I left. "Fine. Take me to the Lucky Leprechaun party."

"You've got it." He sped up a little. "I hear you met my sister and wife."

"Yeah. I didn't appreciate the wild-goose chase they tried to send me on." I took the file out of my purse and laid it on the seat between us. "You can give them back their file."

"I don't think they were sending you on a goose chase. I think they were seeing if you were good enough to do the job." He gave a sideways glance to the file. "I wondered where my file went."

"Your file?" I asked.

"Oh yeah. My wife likes to butt into things. She thinks because I'm the chief, she can come down to the station and just take whatever she wants. Granted"—he turned on what I recognized as the main street— "we've not had a lot of big crimes. But when we do, she likes to have all the insider information because she likes to think she's got a leg up on people. Between me and you, the stuff I don't want out in the public is stored where she can't get to it."

"Are you telling me that you deliberately set stuff out so she will inadvertently tell the public so it'll lead to some gossip which might give you some clues?" I liked his devious little scheme.

"You are a good investigative reporter." He didn't admit to what I'd uncovered, but he didn't deny it either. "Here you go." He stopped at the top of the street where the huge painted leprechaun stood.

Images of Vern, Jay, and Rosey sneaking around in the dark to get the darn thing up put a smile on my face.

"Aren't you coming?" I asked and opened the car door.

"I've got to get my report finished and send Melissa Mann to the state penitentiary to be held. We don't have a big department, and I'd have—" he started to say when I interrupted.

"You'd have to have officers leave the Lucky Leprechaun party." I laughed and got out of the car.

"You're a quick learner. You might just make a good editor at the *Junction Journal* after all." He took off before I could ask him what on earth he was talking about.

"We've been waiting for you." Marge Strickland and her sister Louise were standing on the curb. "There was a young man that came to our house. He said he was with that fancy news station you were interviewing with. He also told us that you weren't doing the investigation. In fact, he said you weren't even hired."

"That's right." Louise nodded. "We did a little digging, and we talked to a Richard Stone. He said that you weren't there on time for the interview, so he hired someone else. But we didn't tell that reporter nothing. Kicked him."

"We had to call Dave to come and peck him to death off our property." Marge tucked her arm into the crook of my arm. "I can see by the look on your face that you're upset. But we have got a good offer for you."

"Rhett said he'd get the online paper and equipment needed for the modern-day online newspaper. We also talked to Garnett and Clara Ness over at the printing press, and they are willing to give us a good deal on a one-day-a-week paper where we'd post things like the obituary and social functions." Louise continued to tell me their plans while Marge walked me down the street.

I listened to them and took in all the vendor booths that hadn't been there when Rhett and I had stopped by his house. There were food vendors touting all sorts of green foods or foods they'd turned green for the occasion, as well as a few local vendors selling things locally made. Leni was one of them.

Vern stood next to his wife and looked at me with a smile when I passed by with the aunts. He lifted his finger up and pointed to the Lucky Leprechaun, then slid it up to his mouth.

His secret was safe with me. Besides, who was I to take away how happy he made the citizens of Holiday Junction as the Merry Maker?

The Lucky Leprechaun had really planned a great party to end the Shamrock Festival.

"Are you going to come work for us or not? We need a real investigative reporter." Marge tugged my arm closer to her body. "Heck, we just need a reporter."

"Wait." I stopped. "Are you trying to tell me that I don't have a job with Richard Stone's network?"

Both of them shook their heads.

"Excuse me." I pulled my arm away from Marge. "I need to make a phone call."

I hurried down the street to the only house I knew, Rhett's. I slipped around the corner of his house to be alone so I could call Richard and out of earshot of the party and the Mad Fiddlers.

"Richard, it's Violet Rhinehammer, international reporter." I stated my truth with a stern voice. "It's my understanding you've sent a colleague of mine to do the reporting for the murder that I happened to solve tonight."

I was going to give him the opportunity to take back what he'd told the aunts about my employment status before I told him exactly where to go.

"I'm afraid the position you've applied for has been filled" was all he had to say.

"You never even gave me a chance." I made sure my tone didn't sound desperate. Then I took a downward spiral. "I packed up my life to come for that interview. I left my home. An amazing job. Friends. Family." I rattled off the list of creature comforts that made me who I was.

"I'm sorry, Ms. Rhinehammer. I'm more than happy to keep your application on file, and when a new reporter position posts, I'll let you know." Richard Stone hung up the phone, closing my dream down.

"I'll fix him." I pulled the phone from my ear and hit the contact button to find Mae West's number.

"Violet!" She greeted me in her oh-so-happy way.

I snarled.

"We are so excited to have found out that you solved the murder. The Laundry Club Ladies, including Dottie Swaggert, were rooting for you. I bet you're so excited! When do you leave for California? When are we going to see you on the big television?"

"About that." I sucked in a deep breath. I jerked around when I heard a branch snap behind me.

Rhett was walking around the back of his house. He looked as surprised to see me as I was him.

"Oh, and before I forget," Mae continued, "they filled your position at the *Normal Gazette*. A big pain in the you-know-what."

My heart dropped. I had been about to tell her I would be on the next airplane back to Normal.

"Since you know about the case being solved, I better let you go. They are having a St. Patrick's Day party, and I don't want to miss it." Mae and I said goodbye, and I turned to Rhett.

"I hear the aunts made you an offer." He didn't have to tell me how he'd heard about my big dream job going up in smoke.

I didn't know him well, but by the way he was acting I could tell he knew and was trying not to show it.

There might have been some underlying issues with Rhett and his family, but underneath it all, I could tell he had a heart. And I didn't really care about their family history. It wasn't my business. Yet.

"Mayor Paisley and I would like to take this time to welcome our new citizen and new reporter at the *Junction Journal*. Give a warm Holiday Junction welcome to Violet Rhinehammer!" Kristine had taken the stage alongside of Mayor Paisley and the aunts. All of them were looking toward Rhett's house.

I smiled and lifted my hand up in the air, wondering what on earth I had just done.

The claps and roars erupted.

"The aunts don't like to take no for an answer." Rhett joined in on the celebration.

I tried not to make eye contact with too many people because I wasn't even sure if I was going to stay here.

As I made my way through the crowd, it was kind of hard not to notice Darren and Rhett Strickland flashing their cute dimples at me, clapping as both of their smiles grew.

The news I would be reporting on for the *Junction Journal* might not be that interesting, but it felt like my personal life was going to be quite the opposite. I was up for a good challenge. Besides, I had no other offer on the table.

Celebrate Mother's Day with Violet Rhinehammer as she joins Holiday Junction as a citizen. And when her mama shows up, southern twang and all, let's just say Mother's Day in Holiday Junction will never be the same.

THE END

If you enjoyed reading this book as much as I enjoyed writing it then be sure to return to the Amazon page and leave a review.

Go to Tonyakappes.com for a full reading order of my novels and while there join my newsletter. You can also find links to Facebook, Instagram and Goodreads.

Keep scrolling to read chapter one from Mother's Day Murder, Book 2 in Holiday Cozy Mystery Series now available to purchase on Amazon.

Chapter One of Book Two
Mother's Day Murder

"Hey! Don't I know you?" It was the first thing I heard before I'd been able to take a sip of the steamy hot cup of coffee I'd gotten from the Brewing Beans, the local coffee shop in Holiday Junction.

I'd not even gotten the toe of my shoe on the first step of the trolley before I heard the familiar voice.

"You!" The trolley driver shook her finger at me.

"Yes. I'm the new reporter for the." I started to rattle off my new job at the Journal Junction the local newspaper. What I didn't say was how I was also the editor for the Talk of the Town article.

That was a long held secret in Holiday Junction that I just so happened to take over recently.

"No. No. No." The visor she wore on her head had blinking lights on it.

Of course it did. Everything in Holiday Junction was either light up, glittered, sparkled or shined. And if it didn't, the residents of the Village made sure it did somehow.

"It's me." She took her hands off the trolley wheel. "Goldie Bennett!"

My eyes narrowed as I looked at her trying to recall any sort of memory of her but I was pulling a blank.

"You know Joey, Chance and Lizzy's grandmother," she said it like I should know these people. "Duh," her mouth was open. "From the airplane. We were seatmates."

"Oh." The horrible memory popped into my head. "Yes. I'm sorry." I held up my cup of Joe. "It's still a little early."

"It's ten o'clock a.m.," she told me like she didn't believe my excuse. "Different strokes for different folks," she muttered and put her hand back on the handle before she said, "Are you riding or not?"

"Yes." I took the last step up into the trolley, barely making it inside before she whipped the door shut nearly catching my heel, which would've hurt if it did get caught since I was wearing flip flops.

right up front next to Goldie.

I eased down, careful not to spill my coffee, and put my briefcase in my lap.

"Well aren't you going to ask about Joey, Chance, and Lizzy?" Goldie asked out of the side of her mouth as the trolley rattled down the Main Street before it hung a left down Peppermint Court, a row of really cute cottage style houses that not only had the feeling of living in the city but also a nice view of the dunes and sliver of the seaside.

"How are your grandchildren?" I was having déjà vu all over again from the first time I'd met Goldie. My hands started to tremble thinking about it.

No. She wasn't terrible to sit by now that I knew was had come after. Of course I was in a different mindset when I stepped on the airplane that morning. I thought I was headed to my dream job in California as a big time new reporter for a national news station. Little did I know when I sat down next to Goldie, I would excuse myself to get away from looking at photos of her grandchildren to go to the bathroom. I had to be in the zone for the shot at the big time but when I found a dead body in the airplane's bathroom, my life took a turn that I never saw coming.

Just like this morning. I never in a million years thought I'd see Goldie again. At least she didn't ask me about the body or worse, seen all the social media memes that'd been created of me after I'd gotten the brilliant, not so brilliant, idea to go live to show off my reporting skills since I was the only reporter in the locked down airport.

Reporter 101 tip, if you do go live on the spot make sure your eye make-up hasn't bled down your face creating a stream of black tears. Not a look viewers want to see.

"You know, we are in full swing of tee-ball. Lizzy. Whooo-wee that Lizzy. She can rock a pink tu-tu better than any of them dancers down at the Groove and Go." She whipped the trolley down a back alley before she took a right back on Main Street so we could head the opposite direction. "Elvin isn't happy with her going down there because he said Tricia Lustig don't need all the money," she tsked. "You know they've got that Lustig Spring everyone goes on and on about."

"Lustig Spring?" I wondered.

The trolley came to an abrupt stop. Goldie leaned to the right and grabbed the handle, pulling the trolley door open.

"Your stop." Her chin swung over her right shoulder and she looked at me.

"Already?" I looked up and saw we were already at the office of the Junction Journal. I stood up about to take those steps off the trolley. "I didn't know I told you where to stop."

"Now, now, Violet." She tsked again, only a little louder this time. "Everyone knows who you are in Junction Journal. They can't say that they really know you like I do."

I stood on the curb staring back at her wondering exactly what that meant.

She slammed the trolley door shut and took off heading to the next stop.

Why not spend your Mother's Day in Holiday Junction and keep up with Violet Rhinehammer as she once again has to put on her sleuthing cap to make sure all the Mothers have a day they deserve!

Mother's Day Murder is now available to purchase on Amazon.

A NOTE FROM TONYA

New to Violet Rhinehammer's journey? She's actually a secondary character from my popular series A Camper & Criminals Cozy Mystery.

She created her own following of readers who loved her and so did I! I happen to love every single holiday and I had an idea to write a holiday series. When I thought of a new sleuth, Violet had popped into my head and she begged me to give her a shot.

I fought her for a couple of months and refused to even think about her leaving the camper series. But she continued to wake me up in the middle of the night, creep into my thought and eventually decided not to show up to my writing sprints for the camper series.

She refused and threw herself a big hissy fit until I gave in. Then I did what I normally do when I start a new series. I began to ask her questions, yes. I do that with my characters.

She thought it would be a good exit from the camper series by getting a phone call where she was going to finally get her chance with a HUGE television network. Then she started laughing and said what if I found a dead body on the airplane where I had to make an emergency landing.

I told her I was listening and to go on....

She said, what if the town was cooky and celebrated every single holiday, then I was stuck there because they wouldn't let planes leave until the murder was solved.

Y'all! I told Violet she was brilliant and the Holiday Cozy Mystery Series was created.

These novels won't be actually released on the holiday during the book because I have a special group on Patreon that are TRUE tonya Kappes FANS. Literally we have a monthly zoom as well as our own book club, daily chats and extra things that will never see the light of any other social media. It's literally like they are writing with me.

As a thank you to them for being them, I actually write on these books every day. After I finish them, I post them. So it's like a daily serial book they can read daily. They also give me feedback and we kinda do it together. It's been a fun time and I have decided to continue doing this until ...well...forever!

If you'd like to read about Violet Rhinehammer in her earlier days before the Holiday Cozy Mystery series, you can check her out in the Camper & Criminals Cozy Mystery.

If you'd like to keep up with Violet every day or just check out our patreon page, you can find it here: https://www.patreon.com/Tonyakappesbooks

XOXO ~ Tonya

www.Tonyakappes.com

BOOKS BY TONYA
SOUTHERN HOSPITALITY WITH A SMIDGEN OF HOMICIDE

Camper & Criminals Cozy Mystery Series

All is good in the camper-hood until a dead body shows up in the woods.

BEACHES, BUNGALOWS, AND BURGLARIES
DESERTS, DRIVING, & DERELICTS
FORESTS, FISHING, & FORGERY
CHRISTMAS, CRIMINALS, AND CAMPERS
MOTORHOMES, MAPS, & MURDER
CANYONS, CARAVANS, & CADAVERS
HITCHES, HIDEOUTS, & HOMICIDES
ASSAILANTS, ASPHALT & ALIBIS
VALLEYS, VEHICLES & VICTIMS
SUNSETS, SABBATICAL AND SCANDAL
TENTS, TRAILS AND TURMOIL
KICKBACKS, KAYAKS, AND KIDNAPPING
GEAR, GRILLS & GUNS
EGGNOG, EXTORTION, AND EVERGREEN
ROPES, RIDDLES, & ROBBERIES
PADDLERS, PROMISES & POISON
INSECTS, IVY, & INVESTIGATIONS
OUTDOORS, OARS, & OATH
WILDLIFE, WARRANTS, & WEAPONS
BLOSSOMS, BBQ, & BLACKMAIL
LANTERNS, LAKES, & LARCENY
JACKETS, JACK-O-LANTERN, & JUSTICE
SANTA, SUNRISES, & SUSPICIONS
VISTAS, VICES, & VALENTINES
ADVENTURE, ABDUCTION, & ARREST
RANGERS, RVS, & REVENGE

CAMPFIRES, COURAGE & CONVICTS
TRAPPING, TURKEY & THANKSGIVING
GIFTS, GLAMPING & GLOCKS
ZONING, ZEALOTS, & ZIPLINES
HAMMOCKS, HANDGUNS, & HEARSAY
QUESTIONS, QUARRELS, & QUANDARY
WITNESS, WOODS, & WEDDING
ELVES, EVERGREENS, & EVIDENCE
MOONLIGHT, MARSHMALLOWS, & MANSLAUGHTER
BONFIRE, BACKPACKS, & BRAWLS

Killer Coffee Cozy Mystery Series

Welcome to the Bean Hive Coffee Shop where the gossip is just as hot as the coffee.

SCENE OF THE GRIND
MOCHA AND MURDER
FRESHLY GROUND MURDER
COLD BLOODED BREW
DECAFFEINATED SCANDAL
A KILLER LATTE
HOLIDAY ROAST MORTEM
DEAD TO THE LAST DROP
A CHARMING BLEND NOVELLA (CROSSOVER WITH MAGICAL
CURES MYSTERY)
FROTHY FOUL PLAY
SPOONFUL OF MURDER
BARISTA BUMP-OFF
CAPPUCCINO CRIMINAL
MACCHIATO MURDER

Holiday Cozy Mystery Series

CELEBRATE GOOD CRIMES!

FOUR LEAF FELONY
MOTHER'S DAY MURDER
A HALLOWEEN HOMICIDE
NEW YEAR NUISANCE
CHOCOLATE BUNNY BETRAYAL
FOURTH OF JULY FORGERY
SANTA CLAUSE SURPRISE
APRIL FOOL'S ALIBI

Kenni Lowry Mystery Series

Mysteries so delicious it'll make your mouth water and leave you hankerin' for more.

FIXIN' TO DIE
SOUTHERN FRIED
AX TO GRIND
SIX FEET UNDER
DEAD AS A DOORNAIL
TANGLED UP IN TINSEL
DIGGIN' UP DIRT
BLOWIN' UP A MURDER
HEAVENS TO BRIBERY

Magical Cures Mystery Series

Welcome to Whispering Falls where magic and mystery collide.

A CHARMING CRIME
A CHARMING CURE
A CHARMING POTION (novella)
A CHARMING WISH

A CHARMING SPELL
A CHARMING MAGIC
A CHARMING SECRET
A CHARMING CHRISTMAS (novella)
A CHARMING FATALITY
A CHARMING DEATH (novella)
A CHARMING GHOST
A CHARMING HEX
A CHARMING VOODOO
A CHARMING CORPSE
A CHARMING MISFORTUNE
A CHARMING BLEND (CROSSOVER WITH A KILLER COFFEE COZY)
A CHARMING DECEPTION

Mail Carrier Cozy Mystery Series

Welcome to Sugar Creek Gap where more than the mail is being delivered.

STAMPED OUT
ADDRESS FOR MURDER
ALL SHE WROTE
RETURN TO SENDER
FIRST CLASS KILLER
POST MORTEM
DEADLY DELIVERY
RED LETTER SLAY

About Tonya

Tonya has written over 100 novels, all of which have graced numerous bestseller lists, including the USA Today. *Best known for stories charged with emotion and humor and filled with flawed characters, her novels have garnered reader praise and glowing critical reviews. She lives with her husband and a very spoiled rescue cat named Ro. Tonya grew up in the small southern Kentucky town of Nicholasville. Now that her four boys are grown men, Tonya writes full-time in her camper she calls her SHAMPER (she-camper).*

Learn more about her be sure to check out her website tonyakappes.com. Find her on Facebook, Twitter, BookBub, and Instagram

Sign up to receive her newsletter, where you'll get free books, exclusive bonus content, and news of her releases and sales.

If you liked this book, please take a few minutes to leave a review now! Authors (Tonya included) really appreciate this, and it helps draw more readers to books they might like. Thanks!

Cover artist: Mariah Sinclair: The Cover Vault

Made in United States
Orlando, FL
08 November 2023

38731061R00088